AF485182

Hellebore Fields

A Dark Academia Hockey Romance

Hellebore Fields

A Dark Academia Hockey Romance

Rivkah Plume

Written by Rivka Plume
Edited **and** Formatted by One Button Publishing

First Edition 2026

ISBN 979-8-9912282-9-9 *(Hardcover)*
Library of Congress Control Number: 2 0 2 5 9 1 9 7 4 2
Printed in the United States of America

Alternate Cover Design by 100 Covers
Interior Cover Art by Tetiana Gut
ISBN: 979-8-9992124-7-4 *(Paperback)*
ISBN: 979-8-9945536-0-2 *(Hardcover)*

For rights and permissions, please contact:
Aber Stoat Publishing, LLC
2173 Salk Ave, Ste 250
Carlsbad, CA. 92008
hello@aberstoatpublishing.com
http://aberstoatpublishing.com @aberstoat

Aber Stoat
PUBLISHING, LLC

Contents

1

Roses and Thorns

Tesni

The lecture hall smells like old books and older regrets. It's a mix of dust and leather that clings to the back of my throat. I shift in my seat, the wooden chair creaking under me. Around me, UC Wisteria's elite students scribble notes or stare blankly at the stained-glass windows. The late afternoon light filters through, tinged with red. The room's pretty fancy, with its vaulted ceiling and rows of desks that look like they've judged a hundred years of students before me. I don't belong here—not really—but I'm damn well going to act like I do.

My fingers trace the edge of my secondhand notebook, the corner already dog-eared from nervous fidgeting. Three weeks into the semester, and I still feel like an imposter. The scholarship girl among trust fund babies. Mom would tell me to hold my head high—you earned this, Tesni—but some days the weight of belonging is heavier than all my textbooks combined.

Professor Hawthorne paces at the front, a rhythm to his steps that almost matches the ticking of the ancient clock above the blackboard. The chalk dust swirling in the air somehow doesn't stick to his dark blazer. He's dissecting some gothic novel I've already read twice, his voice rising and falling like a tide.

"Love," he says, pausing to let the word hang in the air like the dust motes dancing in the colored light, "is it salvation or a delusion?" His eyes sweep the room, and I swear they linger on me a heartbeat too long. My pen taps against my notebook, and I sit straighter.

"I think it's both," I blurt before I can stop myself. The words tumble out, unbidden but honest. Heads turn—Helena Humphries, two rows up, with her perfect blonde bun, smirks like I've just said the dumbest thing ever. I flush, but I'm not backing down. "Love transforms you. It's messy and raw, sure, but it's real. It can pull you out of the dark if you let it."

The memory of Mom's face surfaces—tired after double shifts but still making me birthday cupcakes at midnight, love pushing back against exhaustion. That's what these people don't understand.

Helena snorts, loud enough to echo against the vaulted ceiling. "That's fairy-tale nonsense, Solaris. It's just chemicals and bad decisions." Her voice drips with that upper-crust drawl, the kind that says she's never had to fight for anything. A few others murmur in agreement—cynics, all of them, born with silver spoons in their mouths.

"Maybe for you," I shoot back, heat creeping up my neck. My heart hammers against my ribs. "But I'd rather believe in something than nothing. And the greatest literature—the stuff we're actually studying—suggests I'm right. The transformative power of love is what drives half the canon we worship here." I gesture around the hallowed walls, surprised by my own boldness.

Sophia shifts beside me, her pen pressing hard enough into her paper that I can hear the scratch. She's probably itching to jump in, but I don't look at her. I'm not here to hide.

Professor Hawthorne raises a brow, looking amused. "An optimist in a den of wolves. Interesting." He scribbles something on the board—redemption through affection—and I wonder if he's mocking me or not. "Anyone else care to weigh in?"

A lanky guy near the window raises his hand. "Love's just a construct to sell greeting cards and diamonds." Several people laugh, self-satisfied snickers that make my skin prickle.

A guy in the back, all slouch and hoodie, mutters, "It's a trap. Always is." Laughter ripples through the room, but it's brittle, like they're scared he's right. I roll my eyes. These people don't get it—they've never had to claw their way up from nothing, never needed love to be more than a fling or a footnote.

"So, we're all too sophisticated for genuine emotion now?" I find myself saying, louder than intended. "That's convenient. Pretend nothing matters so you never have to risk anything."

A few surprised glances shoot my way. Even Sophia nudges me with her elbow—a silent *easy there*.

The debate sputters on, voices overlapping, but I tune them out. My gaze drifts to the window, where the campus sprawls beyond—stone arches, ivy choking the walls, a sky bruising purple. DSM-V hums faintly from someone's earbuds nearby, its eerie beat curling into my thoughts. I imagine love like that song—haunting, relentless, pulling you under until you can't tell if you're drowning or flying.

I doodle absently in the margins of my notes—a tangle of hellebore flowers, their blossoms delicate but poisonous. Mom used to warn me about them in our tiny garden. *Beautiful things can still hurt you, Tes.*

Class ends with a shuffle of bags and a scrape of chairs. I'm halfway through shoving my notebook into my backpack when Professor Hawthorne calls my name. "Tesni, a word?" His tone's casual, but there's a weight to it that makes my stomach flip. I nod, slinging my bag over my shoulder, and weave through the exiting crowd.

Helena brushes past, her perfume sharp and expensive, and mutters, "Teacher's pet already?" I grit my teeth, pretending I didn't hear. She's been coming at me since orientation, like my presence is personally offensive to her carefully curated world.

"Don't let her get to you," whispers a girl I barely know—Mina, maybe?—with a sympathetic smile as she passes. I manage a grateful nod before continuing to Professor Hawthorne's desk.

Up close, the professor is even more intimidating—tall, sharp-jawed, with eyes that see too much. "Your argument was...spirited," he says, leaning against his desk. A leather-bound edition of something rare sits beside him, its spine cracked with age. "Naive, perhaps, but bold. You've got a voice. Don't let them silence it."

I blink, caught off guard. I'd expected criticism, not encouragement. "Thanks, I guess? I just—I meant it. Love's worth believing in." I tug at the fraying strap of my bag, suddenly conscious of how worn it looks against the polished wood of his desk.

He smiles, small and cryptic. "Hold on to that. This place has a way of testing ideals." His eyes flick to the window, then back to me. "Your analysis of Shelley was insightful. I'd like to see more of that in your next paper."

Before I can ask what he means, he's turning away, dismissing me with a nod. I linger for a second, then head for the door. My sneakers squeak on the polished floor, embarrassingly loud in the emptying hall.

Outside, the corridor's a chaos of voices and footsteps. The grand hallway stretches ahead, all marble floors and portraits of dead benefactors whose judging eyes seem to follow me. Groups of students cluster together, their laughter bouncing off the stone walls. I weave between them, feeling both invisible and exposed.

A clock somewhere chimes four. I quicken my pace, thinking about the reading I need to finish tonight and the extra shift I picked up at the campus coffee shop. No trust fund to fall back on means no luxury of free time.

I'm almost to the stairwell when I crash into someone—hard. My bag slips, spilling its contents onto the tiles. Pens roll in every direction, and my battered copy of *Wuthering Heights* skids across the floor.

"Shit, sorry—" I start, dropping to grab my stuff, and then I look up.

He's all edges and shadows—dark hair falling into piercing blue eyes, a jaw clenched like he's biting back a curse. Branwen Atthill. I know him from whispers, from the way people part around him like he's a storm coming. His hockey jacket's slung over one shoulder, and he smells like ice and something sharper, maybe smoke. He stares down at me, unblinking, and my chest tightens.

"Watch it," he growls, but he's bending too, snatching a spilled granola bar before I can. His movements are fluid, athletic. A bruise shadows his knuckles, fresh and dark against pale skin. He holds the bar out, fingers brushing mine, and the contact jolts me like static. "You're the girl from class. The love-is-magic one."

I snatch the bar back, heat creeping up my neck. "It's not magic. It's—forget it. You wouldn't get it." My voice sounds steadier than I feel. The hallway seems to have emptied somehow, the noise fading to background murmurs.

His lips twitch, not quite a smile. "Try me." His voice is low, rough, like he's daring me to keep talking. I should walk away—Sophia's warning flares in my head: *He's trouble, Tes. Stay clear.* But my feet don't move. There's something in his stare, hungry and unguarded, that hooks me.

"Fine. Love isn't magic—it's work. It's showing up every day and choosing someone even when it's hard." I shove my book back in my bag. "It's...standing in their darkness and being their light when they can't find it themselves." The words feel too personal suddenly, like I'm revealing too much.

He studies me, something flickering behind those ice-blue eyes. "Sounds exhausting." But there's a question in his tone, like he's testing me.

"Worth it, though," I counter, straightening up. Our faces are closer than I expected, and I notice a tiny scar bisecting his left eyebrow. "Everything worthwhile is."

"Tesni!" Sophia's voice cuts through, sharp and annoyed. She's barreling toward me, her curly hair bouncing, eyes narrowing at Branwen. "We're late for coffee. Let's go."

I hesitate, glancing at him. He doesn't budge; he just watches me like I'm a puzzle he's already solving. Something dangerous and thrilling coils in my stomach.

"See you around," he says, and it sounds like a promise. Then he's gone, disappearing into the crowd, leaving me clutching my bag and wondering why my heart's still racing.

Sophia grabs my arm, tugging me toward the stairs. "What the hell was that? You know who he is, right?"

"Yeah," I mutter, but I'm barely listening. My skin's still buzzing where his fingers grazed mine, and I can't shake the feeling that something just shifted—something I'm not sure I can undo. "I know what people say."

"It's not just what people say, Tes." Her voice drops to a whisper as we descend the stairs. "The fights, the suspensions...last year he put a guy in the hospital during a game. On purpose."

"Two sides to every story," I say, though doubt creeps in.

"Not when one side has a lacerated spleen."

I roll my eyes; histrionic as always.

Sophia stops on the landing, forcing me to look at her. "This is exactly what I mean. You always want to see the best in people, even when there's no 'best' to see." Her face softens. "Just...be careful, okay? Not everyone's worth trying to save."

I nod, but as we push through the heavy doors into the crisp autumn air, I glance back, and through the window, I catch a glimpse of him watching me from the top of the stairs—like a shadow against the golden light of the hall.

Maybe Sophia's right. Maybe he is dangerous.

But then again, so are all the best stories.

2

Ice and Obsession

Branwen

The cold digs into my knuckles as I slam my stick against the boards, the crack echoing through the arena like a gunshot. Sweat stings my eyes, and my breath punches out in short, white bursts that hang in the frigid air. Practice is a complete mess—pucks flying wide, Jenkins tripping over himself, Coach Hendricks yelling until his voice cracks. I don't care.

My head's stuck on that "Love is everything" girl. Tesni. With her soft hair and that damn voice, all bright and hopeful, cutting through like it owns the place. *Love transforms you.* It's total bullshit—so why the hell is it looping in my brain like a scratched record?

"Atthill! Get your head out of the fucking clouds!" Hendricks' shout bounces off the ice. I skate a hard loop, blades biting deep into the fresh-cut surface, leaving twin trails of white behind me. The team's a blur of navy and silver—Jenkins, Milo, Forester, the rest—grunting and chasing the drill like the good little soldiers they are. I'm supposed to set the tone, show the rookies how it's done.

But I'm off. I keep seeing her in that hallway, pens rolling, glaring up at me like I'd ruined her day. She's too warm, too earnest...but it feels real. I don't get how anyone can see the world—let alone the idea of love—through such rosy glasses.

"D-line shift! Atthill, take the point!" Hendricks barks from the bench.

I slide into position, tapping my stick on the ice. The center feeds me the puck and I cradle it against my blade. The defensive setup forms in front of me—two forwards trying to block my shot and a center hovering, waiting to intercept. I feign left, then fire a shot. The puck slams the crossbar with a metallic ring that echoes through the arena.

"Holy shit!" Milo yelps as the puck ricochets dangerously close to his face. "Chill, Bran—we're on *your* team, bro." He's whiny, a sophomore who still thinks he can yap at me just because his dad's on the board of trustees. I glare daggers at him and he shuts his trap, skating backward a few feet.

"Watch your stick, Atthill," Jenkins mutters, skating past. His shoulder deliberately clips mine. "Last time you snapped one, Coach red-assed *me* for it." He's half-joking, but I know he's still pissed about that fight last season when I broke that UW player's collarbone. Clean hit, everyone said. Well, except for me—I knew exactly what I was doing.

I don't answer Jenkins—just spit on the ice and keep moving. We run three more drills: breakaways, penalty kills, and finally, a scrimmage that turns ugly when I check Forester hard into the boards. Not my fault he can't take a hit.

The whistle shrieks; practice is over. I rip off my helmet, shaking out damp hair, and head for the tunnel. My legs ache from the suicides Coach made us run after I "accidentally" high-sticked Milo, but it's not enough to drown out the noise in my head. The locker room hits me with the smell of sweat and body spray, steam rolling from the showers. *Despicable* growls low from Milo's crap speaker, the bass sinking into my chest, and it fits—my mood, this dump, everything.

I drop onto the bench, yank at my laces, and grab my phone. There she is. The photo. Took it last week outside the library. She's hunched over a book, hair falling in her face—zero clue I was there. I've got three more candids just like it: Tesni crossing the quad; laughing with that friend of hers; waiting in line at the coffee shop. I zoom in on the library one. She's mine—she just doesn't know how yet. That light she's got—it's like a hit I didn't know I was chasing.

"Bran, you good?" Jenkins looms over me, towel around his neck, grinning too wide. His hair's still dripping from the shower, water beading on his shoulders. I shove the phone in my pocket.

"Fuck off," I snap, jerking my skate loose with more force than necessary. He laughs, stepping back, but his eyes dig in, nosy as hell.

"Someone's touchy. Girl trouble?" He chuckles at his lame-ass joke, and my fist clenches so tight my knuckles crack.

"Say that again." I stand, crowding him, voice low. His grin falters, that confident captain bullshit fading when he remembers who he's talking to. Too many soft kids around here used to guys with bark and no bite.

"Easy, man. Chill." He retreats, grabbing his bag, but I don't let it go that easy. My heart's pounding, vision narrowing. He's lucky I don't knock his teeth into his throat.

"You watching me, Jenkins?" I step closer. "Got something to say, say it."

"Relax, Atthill." He holds up his hands. "Take a breath. Do some fucking yoga. It's hockey—you fight the *other* team. Not everything's a fight."

But everything is. That's what none of them get.

I turn to my locker, popping it open. A folded paper slips out, fluttering to the floor—blank, no writing. Weird. I kick it aside, but it bugs me. Is someone messing with my stuff? My jaw tightens, and I glance around. Milo's fiddling with his speaker; the freshman goalie's scrubbing gear in the sink. No one's looking my way. Still, I feel it—eyes on me, somewhere.

Hendricks stomps in, clipboard in hand, face red like it gets when he's been chewing nicotine gum too long. "Atthill, c'mere." He jerks his chin to the corner. I groan, toss my skate down, and follow. The guys pretend not to watch, but I catch Jenkins' smirk. Asshole.

Hendricks crosses his arms, staring me down. His UC Wisteria Hockey jacket stretches tight across his shoulders—he still looks like he could play, even at fifty. "You were a head case out there. Reckless. Sloppy. Those scouts from Boston won't come back if you keep this shit up. What's going on?"

"Nothing," I say. "Just a bad day."

"Bullshit. Something's been off with you ever since the semester started. Talk, or I'll make you sit Saturday's game."

My jaw clenches. Saturday's against our rivals, EC Thornfield. I've got a score to settle with their captain. "You wouldn't bench me for the rivalry game."

"Wanna find out how fast I would?" His eyes narrow. "I've dealt with hotshots before. You think you're special because you've got the best wrist shot in Division I? Get over yourself. Everyone at the next level was hot shit in college; takes 'em a few broken ribs to figure out they're rooks. I'm trying to save you from yourself."

"Why do you care?" I step closer. "You know what? Bench me. See how the alums who pay your bonus feel about losing to Thornfield."

His jaw clenches, a vein bulging at his temple. "Don't push me, kid. Fix this—whatever it is. Don't throw away a real future over whatever bullshit's eating you."

"So, I am starting, then." I smirk, daring him. He looks like he might swing, and part of me wants him to. At least pain would make me feel something other than...this. Lost in the weeds, over some girl I don't even know.

He doesn't. Just shakes his head. "You're throwing it all away, Branwen. Your shot at the pros, the scholarship—don't say I didn't warn you." He turns, muttering about wasted talent, and I'm left there, fists balled, his words sticking like mud.

Back at my locker, I peel off my pads, the damp fabric clinging to my skin. My shoulder throbs where I took that hit during the scrimmage. I'll have a bruise tomorrow. The room's thinning; Milo's gone, Jenkins too, just a few freshmen voices bouncing from the showers. I grab my jacket but pause, fishing out the phone again.

Tesni's face glows on the screen, and my pulse kicks up. She's got no idea how badly she's fucking with my life—and the control I have over it. I trace her jaw with my thumb, imagining her closer, next to me, thinking about what I'd like to do to her. I've watched her for weeks now, learning her schedule and habits like a creep. The coffee shop she hits before morning classes. The bench she likes by the humanities building. How she always has a granola bar in her bag; the cheap kind, like money's tight—hell, I would know.

Tomorrow, if she's in class. I'll be there, right up front, and this time, I'll really talk to her, *make* her see me. She's not slipping away from me.

I pull up my campus schedule app and find the "Sports Literature and Psychology" class Professor Hawthorne announced. Perfect—I'll get myself paired with her for that project. Shouldn't be too hard; no one else ever wants to work with me anyway.

I shove the phone away and head out, grabbing my hockey stick. The hall's empty, my boots echoing on concrete. The rink's quiet now. I walk out onto the empty surface, feeling the cold rise through my boots. This is the only place that makes sense sometimes—sixty by thirty meters of frozen certainty; rules I understand; pain that's straightforward.

I wind up and take a shot at the empty net, the puck sailing into the back corner. Then another. And another. Each one is perfect and controlled. That's how I need everything to be: within my control. Otherwise, it just slips away—or I push it away.

Outside, the air's sharp, slicing through the heat in my chest. I light a cigarette, smoke curling into the dusk, and start walking across the parking lot toward my apartment. Something moves in the corner of my eye—a shadow by the bleachers, I freeze, squinting, but it's nothing. Just the wind, probably, but my skin still prickles. I take a long drag, shaking it off.

She's out there—studying, breathing, being—and I'm here, plotting how to pull her in. It's fucked up—restraining order-level shit–and I know that. But I don't care. She's going to be mine.

I pull out my phone again, bringing up her Insta, which she keeps public, thankfully. Not much there—she's private, cautious. Smart girl. But I've found ways around that. I scroll through what I've gathered, memorizing details. Her hometown. The coffee shop where she works part-time. Her class schedule I pieced together from "accidental" run-ins.

The song from practice is still stuck in my head—*Despicable*. Yeah. That's what I am. But she doesn't need to know that yet. Not until she's in too deep to run.

I flick the cigarette away, watching the ember die on the asphalt. Tomorrow, I'll see her again. Tomorrow, I'll make her notice me. Tomorrow, I'll start making her mine.

Because that light she has? I need it. And what I need, I take.

3

Paired Fates

Tesni

I arrive early, clutching my coffee like it's a lifeline. Last night was another late shift at the campus café, followed by hours of reading. My eyes burn, but I'm here. I'm always here.

The morning light filters through the leaded glass windows of Professor Hawthorne's classroom, painting golden patterns across the worn wooden desks.

I slide into my usual seat, third row from the front—close enough to show I care, far enough to avoid being called on constantly. Sophia won't be in class today; she's presenting at some psychology symposium across campus. Her absence leaves me feeling oddly exposed.

Students trickle in gradually, their voices a soft murmur that fills the room. Helena enters with her usual entourage, their cashmere sweaters and pearls a stark contrast to my thrift store cardigan. Our eyes meet, and she smirks before taking her seat two rows ahead. I ignore her, focusing on organizing my notes from the previous class.

The room goes quiet as someone new enters. I don't need to look up to know who it is—the shift in energy is palpable. But I do look up, and there he is. Branwen. He's never attended this class before, at least not while I've been here. His dark hair falls across his forehead, slightly damp like he's just showered. The hockey jacket is gone today, replaced by a black henley that stretches across his broad shoulders. There's a fresh bruise on his right cheekbone.

My breath catches as he walks directly toward me. Students shift in their seats, watching with poorly disguised interest. He stops at the empty desk beside mine, his blue eyes meeting mine with an intensity that makes my skin warm.

"This taken?" His voice is low, meant only for me despite our audience.

"It's a free country," I answer, aiming for casual but missing by a mile. My voice comes out breathier than intended.

He slides into the seat, the wooden chair creaking under his weight. He smells like mint and something earthy. I'm suddenly hyper-aware of how close he is, close enough that I can see the tiny scar bisecting his eyebrow and the shadow of stubble along his jaw.

"I've seen you around," I say, arranging my pens in a neat row to avoid looking at him.

He leans back with that ever-confident mien. "Yeah...heard it's good."

"You mean you heard you'll get an A because you play a sport?" The question slips out before I can stop it.

His lips curve into something almost like a smile. "It won't hurt."

"I think you might be in for a rude awakening."

"We both might be in for awakenings."

What in the actual fuck does *that* mean? Before I can ask, Professor Hawthorne sweeps in, his tweed jacket worn at the elbows, a leather messenger bag slung across his shoulder. The room falls silent immediately. Even Helena straightens in her seat.

"Good morning," Professor Hawthorne says, his voice carrying to the back row without effort. He surveys the room, pausing briefly on Branwen before continuing. "Today marks the beginning of our interdisciplinary project with the Sports Psychology department. Literature and athletics; they might seem worlds apart but share remarkable parallels."

He begins pacing. "Athletes, like some of the most iconic characters in literature, face internal and external conflicts. 'To be or not to be.' To take the shot or pass it off to a teammate..."

We both might be in for awakenings. There's something about this—him—that sends my hackles up.

"They experience triumph and defeat," Professor Hawthorne continues. "They struggle with identity and navigate complex relationships." He stops, turning to face us. "Your task is to explore these parallels through a semester-long project."

A murmur ripples through the class. Professor Hawthorne raises a hand, silencing it instantly.

"You'll work in pairs—one literature focus, one sports focus. Together, you'll develop a thesis exploring how literary themes manifest in athletic pursuits, and vice versa."

My heart quickens. Group projects are usually my nightmare—I end up doing most of the work while someone else takes half the credit. But this one sounds genuinely interesting, even if I do end up doing all the work; and, if I'm paired with some jock who saw the word "Sport" and signed up, that's pretty much guaranteed.

"I've taken the liberty of assigning pairs based on your academic backgrounds," Professor Hawthorne continues, pulling out a sheet of paper. "When I call your names, please find your partner and take a seat next to them."

He begins reading off pairs, and I listen with increasing anxiety as names that aren't mine fill the air. Helena is paired with Jenkins—a hockey player with a reputation almost as notorious as Branwen's. She looks pleased as punch.

"Tesni Solaris," Professor Hawthorne finally calls, and I sit up straighter. "You'll be working with Branwen Atthill."

The room goes quiet. A few students turn to look at us, expressions ranging from curiosity to pity. I feel Branwen shift beside me, his posture relaxing as if he'd been holding tension I hadn't noticed.

"Lucky me," he says, just loud enough for me to hear.

Is it luck? Hawthorne's gaze meets mine briefly, and I wonder if there's something deliberate in his pairing. I've been vocal in his class, and my essays have earned his praise. Did he think I could...handle Branwen? Or is this some academic science experiment—pair the scholarship girl with the hockey star and see what happens?

"For the remainder of class, meet with your partners to discuss potential project directions," Professor Hawthorne instructs. "I expect an outline by next week."

Chairs scrape as students rearrange themselves. Beside me, Branwen doesn't move; he is already exactly where he needs to be. I turn to face him, trying to look professional despite the nervous flutter in my stomach.

"So," I begin, opening my notebook to a fresh page. "Any thoughts on the project?"

His eyes track the movement of my hand as I write the date at the top of the page. "A few."

"Care to share them?" I prompt when he doesn't continue.

He leans forward, closing some of the distance between us. "You're the lit expert. I'll follow your lead."

"That's not how partnerships work," I counter. "Have you ever read a book with no pictures?"

Something flickers in his eyes that makes me acutely aware of why everyone seems to stay out of his way.

"I might surprise you."

"Okay," I say. "Surprise me, then. What interests you most about literature?"

He considers this, eyes never leaving my face. "Obsession."

The word hangs in the air between us. I write it down, refusing to show how it affects me.

"Obsession," I repeat, keeping my voice steady. "That's definitely a theme we could explore. Gatsby's obsession with Daisy, Heathcliff's with Catherine. There are parallels in sports psychology, I'm sure."

"Plenty," he agrees. "Athletes get fixated on winning; on perfection." His fingers drum against the desk. "It's all-consuming—the chase."

Something in his tone sends a shiver down my spine—not unpleasant, but a warning nonetheless. I press on.

"We could examine how obsession drives performance but ultimately leads to destruction—in both literature and sports." I'm in familiar territory now, academic analysis is providing safe ground—for which I'm grateful, because I don't feel safe. "The fine line between dedication and pathology."

He watches me with an intensity that throws me for a loop, making me wonder if we're still talking about the project. "The line isn't as thin as people think. Sometimes you cross it before you even know it's there."

From across the room, I notice Helena watching us with a sour expression. She doesn't look away; she just raises an eyebrow. I'm not sure what to make of that. I was expecting something snarky, but she almost looks...concerned?

"Should we exchange numbers?" I ask, returning to practicalities. "Just for project coordination."

A smile plays at the corners of his mouth, transforming his face momentarily. "If you insist." He holds out his hand for my phone.

I hesitate only briefly before unlocking it and passing it to him. His fingers brush mine in the exchange. The contact is brief but electric. He types quickly, then hands it back.

"I added my number," he says. "Text me so I have yours."

I nod, sending a *It's Tesni, your project partner* message before realizing that he's saved himself under "Partner". His phone buzzes in his pocket, but he doesn't check it, eyes still fixed on me.

"So," I say, feeling suddenly awkward under his sustained attention. "Should we meet outside of class to work on this? Library maybe?"

"My place would be better," he says. "Quieter."

"Quieter than a place that has a 'no talking' sign on every wall?"

"Not everyone follows the rules like you," he says, and there's something beneath his voice that, in that moment, is alarming and enticing in equal measure.

I snap out of it. Alarm bells ring faintly in my head as Sophia's warnings echo: *He's trouble, Tes.*

"Library first," I counter firmly. "Then we'll see."

"Whatever works for you, Tesni."

The way he says my name rolls off his tongue, it almost sounds like he's been practicing it. I push that strange thought away, focusing on scheduling.

"Tomorrow afternoon? I work until four, but I'm free after."

"I got practice 'til five. How's six?"

I nod my assent, making a note in my planner. "Reference section, sixth floor. It's usually pretty empty."

The rest of the class is spent discussing project parameters. Professor Hawthorne circles the room, like a shark with no real purpose except to move forward. But when he reaches our desk, he pauses, studying our notes.

"Obsession as a destructive force," he reads from my page. "Interesting angle. You might also consider its creative potential—how the same force that destroys can create the chance for extraordinary achievement."

After he moves on, Branwen leans closer. "He gets it."

"Gets what?"

"That obsession isn't always a bad thing." His voice drops lower. "Sometimes it's...necessary."

Class ends before I can respond. As students gather their things, I notice Helena approaching, her face absent its usual smarmy expression.

"Tesni," she says, her voice honey-sweet and just as sticky. "Look at you, getting the hockey star. I'd watch myself if I were you." Her eyes flick to Branwen, who's still seated beside me. "Some of those guys are known for their...roughness."

"I think I can handle myself in the library," I reply, matching her saccharine tone. "But I *so* appreciate your concern."

Branwen stands slowly, unfolding to his full height. He doesn't say anything, but his presence alone seems to make Helena reconsider whatever else she planned to say.

"We'll see," she murmurs before turning away. "Just don't say I didn't warn you. The athletes here can get away with anything they want."

As she walks away, Branwen's hand settles briefly on my shoulder. The weight is surprising, warm and solid.

"Don't let her get to you," he says, echoing the words of that stranger from yesterday. "People like her are threatened by people like you."

"People like me?" I ask, looking up at him.

"Real and unaffected," he says. "Her? She thinks she's the sun in everyone's sky. See you tomorrow, Tesni. Six o'clock."

He leaves without waiting for my response, navigating between desks with surprising grace for someone his size. I watch him go, aware of the eyes that follow him—and, by extension, me.

As I gather my things, Professor Hawthorne approaches my desk. "Ms. Solaris, a moment?"

I nod, wondering if he's having second thoughts about our pairing.

"I'm aware of Branwen Atthill's reputation," he says. "But I believe this partnership could benefit you both. His perspective will challenge yours, and your academic rigor will provide him structure."

"You didn't pair us randomly," I observe.

Professor Hawthorne's lips quirk. "I never do anything randomly, Ms. Solaris." He adjusts his glasses. "I'm sure I needn't remind you that the most compelling characters in literature are often the most damaged. They require careful handling."

"I'm not handling him," I protest. "We're just project partners."

"Of course," he agrees, though his expression suggests he knows more than he's saying. "I look forward to seeing what you create together."

As I leave the classroom, my phone buzzes with a text.

Looking forward to tomorrow. Don't be late. —B

I stare at the message, unsettled by its commanding tone. He doesn't even know me and he's talking to me like that. I think about asking Professor Hawthorne if I can switch partners, but another text follows almost immediately:

Please ;)

I start to smile despite myself, but the red flags with this guy are too bright to ignore, despite his attempts at charm—and the fact that, yes, his physical attributes are...appealing. But I don't have time for distractions.

I slip the phone into my pocket without responding and step out into the crisp autumn air. He may have his hockey pads, but I have guards of my own, and no one gets past them.

4

Shadows and Schemes

Branwen

The library's main reading room has a quiet energy about it—students hunched over laptops, the rustle of turning pages, and the occasional cough echoing off the vaulted ceiling. I stay between tall bookshelves, far enough away that she won't spot me but close enough to hear every word.

Tesni sits at a table near the west windows, the golden afternoon light catching her hair. She's with that friend of hers—Sophia, I think—their heads bent together over coffee cups and open textbooks.

I should be at practice. Coach Hendricks will have my ass for skipping before the big game, but right now, this feels more important.

I adjust my position, sliding behind a shelf of literary criticism. A folded note digs into my pocket—blank, just like the one that fell from my locker yesterday. I found it tucked under my door this morning.

Someone's playing a weird game; I'd care more if I wasn't busy playing my own.

"...*seriously* concerning, Tes," Sophia's voice carries to me. "Branwen Atthill isn't just another dumb jock. He's dangerous. Like, for real, for real."

My jaw tightens. This busybody thinks she knows me. Thinks she can warn Tesni away.

"You don't know him," Tesni argues, her voice softer but firm. "Besides, it's just a project. It's not like he invited me to Winter Formal."

"Hawthorne should know better. Everyone knows what happened last year with that player from Eastern College."

I lean against the bookshelf, memories flashing: The crack of bone beneath my fist; blood spreading across the ice like some gothic painting; how everything went quiet in my head for once.

"That was a hockey fight," Tesni says. "They happen all the time. Haven't you heard that expression? 'I went to a fight, and a hockey game broke out.' It's part of the sport."

Sophia leans forward, lowering her voice. I strain to hear. "It wasn't just a fight, Tes. The kid had to have reconstructive surgery. And there are...other stories. *Off* the ice. Girls who—"

"Stop," Tesni cuts her off. "I'm a grown woman, Soph; I can judge him for myself."

Something warm unfurls in my chest. She's defending me. Doesn't even know me, but she's giving me a chance. It's more than most people do.

"That's exactly what worries me," Sophia sighs. "You're always looking for the best in people. But sometimes, there is no best to find—just red flags you're choosing to ignore."

A student brushes past me, giving me a curious look. I pull a random book from the shelf, pretending to browse. The cover reads *Obsessive Love: When It Hurts Too Much to Let Go*. Now that's an interesting coincidence. If I believed in fate, I'd think this was that, but I don't—fate and control don't mix.

"I can handle myself," Tesni insists. "And honestly, he seems...I don't know. There's something kinda...interesting about him."

Interesting. Okay. I've been called a lot worse.

"Yeah, that's called 'danger vibes,'" Sophia retorts. "Promise me you'll be careful. Meet in public places. Do *not* go to his apartment—or anywhere alone with him."

"Yes, Mom." Tesni laughs. "I'll make sure to get some pepper spray, too."

My fingers curl into a fist. Another obstacle. Another person trying to keep her from me. I make a mental note: Sophia needs to be managed. Discredited, maybe. I've got time to figure it out.

Their conversation shifts to other topics—a paper due next week, a party happening Friday. I tune it out, focusing on Tesni's movements—how she tucks her hair behind her ear when she's thinking, how she doodles in the margins of her notebook—small details I'm collecting, hoarding like precious things.

My phone vibrates. Coach, again. Third call in an hour. I silence it. Practice can wait. Everything outside of this room can wait.

After nearly an hour, Sophia leaves for a class. Tesni stays, spreading her books across the table now that she has it to herself. I wait five minutes, then seven, making sure Sophia is gone before I make my move.

I circle around to approach from the main entrance as if I've just arrived. Tesni doesn't notice me until I'm standing at her table.

She looks up and jolts. I can tell she's not only surprised, but trying to glean whether I overheard her little convo, but I don't give anything away.

"Oh, uh, hi, Branwen. Sorry, did I—I thought we were meeting tomorrow?"

"Had some time," I say with a shrug. "Thought I'd get a head start on research."

She eyes my empty hands. "Without books or a laptop?"

I smile, dropping into the chair across from her. "I'm more of a verbal processor, you know? I like to talk things through first."

Which would mean I would have to know she was going to be here...shit. I'm trying to think of an exit strategy when she closes the book she was reading and offers me one: "Okay. What did you want to talk about?"

"Us," I say, enjoying how the word makes her eyes widen ever-so-slightly. "Our project, I mean." Though that's not what I meant at all.

"Right." She taps her pen against her notebook. "I've been thinking about our obsession angle. There's a lot of material there, especially if we compare literary obsession to sports psychology concepts."

I lean forward, breathing in the scent of her shampoo. It's floral. "Tell me more."

She launches into an explanation of fixation in literature, citing examples from books I've never read but now intend to. I watch her hands as she talks, the way they move to emphasize points. There's a small ink stain on her hand and I resist the urge to touch it.

"What about you?" she asks eventually.

"I'm an open book," I say with a smile, proud of myself for the corny but on-the-spot line.

"I mean, do you have any insights to share from the sports side?"

I consider what to share. How much to reveal. "In hockey, obsession shows up differently. It's all about control—controlling the puck, the play, your opponent. Knowing your own body well enough to control it." I reflexively flex my hand, remembering the feeling of knuckles splitting on Davis's face mask. "But it's a balance. Too much control, you overthink. Not enough, you're reckless."

"And which are you?" she asks, studying me with those brown eyes.

The question catches me off guard. No one asks me about myself, not really. They think they already know. "Depends on the day," I answer honestly. "On the ice, I'm calculated. Every move is planned." Off the ice is another matter entirely...

"And off the ice?" she asks, as if reading my thoughts.

I hold her gaze. Her eyes are bright, but they have depths that hold uncertainty. Sadness. Loneliness.

"I'm still kind of figuring that out," I say.

She opens her mouth to reply, then looks away; it's like she's censoring herself. I hate that for her. And I'm gonna take away that uncertainty.

"I have class," she says, glancing at her watch.

"Let me walk you," I say, already standing.

She hesitates, then nods. "Sure. Thanks."

As she gathers her things, I notice a book peeking from her bag. It's a worn copy of *Wuthering Heights*. I've heard of it but never read it. "That any good?" I ask, gesturing to the book.

She glances down, then smiles—the first real smile she's given me. It transforms her face, and something in my chest tightens painfully. "It's my favorite, actually. How about you? What's yours?"

I shake my head. "Not much of a reader."

"It's about obsession, actually," she says, tucking it deeper into her bag. "Heathcliff's love for Catherine destroys them both. It's a...beautiful disaster."

"Sounds familiar," I murmur, but she doesn't seem to hear me.

We walk across campus together. Students turn to watch us pass—the scholarship girl and the hockey player. An unlikely pair. I notice how she fidgets under their stares, uncomfortable with the attention. She'll need to get over that; all in good time.

"Ignore them," I tell her. "They don't matter."

"Easy for you to say. You're used to it."

"Comes with the territory, but that doesn't mean I like it."

We reach the humanities building, and I stop at the bottom of the steps. "Still on for tomorrow? Six o'clock?"

She nods. "Reference section. Sixth floor."

"I'll be there." I hesitate, then add, "Thanks for defending me. To your friend."

Her eyes widen. "How did you—"

"Libraries are quiet, remember?" I offer a smile, hoping she won't read too much into the fact that I'd still have to have been eavesdropping. Before she can question me further, I hop off the steps. "See you tomorrow, Tesni."

I walk away, feeling her gaze on my back. Only when I'm sure she's gone inside do I cut across the quad toward my apartment. Coach will be livid that I missed practice, but I'll deal with that tomorrow. Tonight, I have plans to make.

My apartment sits on the edge of campus—a perk of my hockey scholarship. Most of the team lives in the athletic dorms, but I negotiated for privacy when I was choosing schools. Needed my own space, away from their constant noise and bullshit bonding.

The place is sparse—bed, desk, and a kitchenette I rarely use. Hockey gear is piled in one corner. A wall of photos above my desk, mostly game shots from last season. And now, two new additions: Tesni in the library. Tesni walking across the quad.

I drop onto my bed, pulling out my phone. No messages from her yet about tomorrow. I scroll through my contacts, stopping at Jenkins' name. He could be useful—he knows Helena, who clearly has issues with Tesni. Might be worth exploiting that connection.

A blank white envelope catches my eye, propped against my laptop. My pulse quickens as I tear it open. Another empty sheet, just like the others. But this time, there's a faint mark—the impression of writing pressed from another page. I hold it to the light, tracing the indentation with my finger. It looks like the letter H.

Someone's definitely fucking with me. Part of me wants to crumple it, forget it. The other part—the part that catalogs threats, that never lets anything slide—tucks it away with the others. Three now. Patterns matter.

I pull up a file labeled "Color Palettes - Art Class" from a random folder buried in my system utilities; the kind of document no one would think to check. It's full of Tesni's info, pulled from public sources (her scholarship group was interviewed about their work-study programs), her social media, and the records I've kept of her routine—classes, shifts at the coffee shop.

My phone buzzes, and I grab it, hoping it's her, but it's Hendricks:

Miss another practice and you're benched Saturday. Not fucking around here.

I ignore it, opening another file—this one labeled "Notes - 3/21 - History" and stored in a different anonymous folder—instead. I've outlined three potential meeting locations: the library (her choice), the campus coffee shop where she works (familiar territory for her, easy to extend meetings due to her comfort level), and eventually, my apartment (privacy, control, the end goal).

Six weeks until the project's due. Six weeks to make her dependent on me for academic success, and isolate her from Sophia and anyone else who might interfere. The plan unfolds in my mind; I know the whole thing is twisted. I know I'm crossing lines. But I don't care. In the end, even she'll agree that it was all worth it.

My phone buzzes again, and this time, it is her.

Still good for tomorrow, 6 pm? But on second thought, let's do the café instead. I'll bring the Victorian lit examples if you can cover the sports psychology side. —Tesni

I stare at the message and the way she signs her name on a text message. So formal and proper. She has no idea what's coming.

I reply: *Looking forward to it, I'll be there.*

I set the phone down, leaning back against the wall. The blank notes, Sophia's warnings, Helena's hostility—all obstacles I'll need to navigate. But I've always been good at finding openings in seemingly impenetrable defenses. It's what makes me valuable on the ice. I know how to navigate my way around obstacles. Or make them go away.

And now, I'm bringing that same focus to Tesni Solaris. She thinks we're just project partners. She thinks she's in control. But by the time she realizes the truth, it'll be too late for her to walk away.

I close my eyes, picturing her face, her voice defending me to Sophia. *I'll judge him for myself.* So trusting. So perfect.

So naive.

5

Fractured Trust

Tesni

Rain taps against the café windows, turning the world beyond into a watercolor blur. I arrived fifteen minutes early to secure the corner table—the one with the mismatched armchairs and the vintage lamp that casts a warm glow against the dreary day. The first draft of our project outline sits before me, my handwriting covering the page with more questions than answers.

"Is this seat taken?"

I look up to find Professor Hawthorne standing beside my table, rain dotting the shoulders of his tweed jacket. I've never seen him in the Broken Spine Café before.

"No, please," I gesture to the empty chair. "Though I'm meeting someone soon."

He settles into the seat, placing his leather satchel on the floor beside him. "Mr. Atthill, I presume?" His eyes hold that same knowing look from class, like he's several chapters ahead in a book we're reading together.

I nod, suddenly self-conscious about my choice of meeting place. The café sits halfway between campus and the athletic facilities—neutral territory that felt safer than the isolated sixth floor of the library.

"How is the project progressing?" Professor Hawthorne asks, signaling to the barista.

"We're still in the research phase," I reply, closing my notebook. "Narrowing our focus."

He smiles faintly. "And how are you finding your partnership?"

The question seems loaded with subtext I can't quite decipher. "Great," I answer with a smile. "Branwen has some great insights; I'm not much of an athlete."

Professor Hawthorne nods as if I've confirmed something. "The most compelling analyses often arise from tension between collaborators." He accepts a steaming mug from the approaching server with a murmured thanks. "Do remember, Ms. Solaris, that academic curiosity should be tempered with personal boundaries."

Before I can ask what *that's* supposed to mean, the café door swings open. Branwen enters, bringing with him the smell of fresh rain. His gaze finds me immediately, then narrows at the sight of Professor Hawthorne.

"Professor," he says as he reaches our table.

"Mr. Atthill." Professor Hawthorne rises smoothly. "I was just leaving. Don't let me interrupt your work." He gathers his satchel and then pauses. "My office hours are extended this week, should you need anything."

The offer feels significant, though I'm not sure why. I nod, watching as he weaves between tables toward the exit. When I look back, Branwen has claimed Professor Hawthorne's vacated seat, his expression unreadable.

"Checking in on you?" he asks, shrugging off his damp jacket. "Making sure you aren't at the risk of any bad influence?"

He chuckles away the last comment, but I think he was dead serious.

"Just a coincidence," I say, though I'm not entirely convinced. "He wanted to know how the project was going."

Branwen's knee brushes mine under the table. The contact sends an unexpected jolt through me. "What'd you tell him?"

"The truth. That we're still figuring things out." I push my notebook toward him. "I made some preliminary notes on literary examples."

He glances at them but doesn't take the notebook. Instead, he studies me with an intensity that makes my skin warm. "You look tired."

The observation catches me off guard. "Double shift yesterday," I admit. "Then a late night with an essay for Armstrong's class."

Something flickers in his eyes. Irritation? "You work too much."

"Some of us have to," I reply, more sharply than intended. "Not everyone has a full scholarship."

His jaw tightens fractionally. "You think I don't work for what I have?"

"That's not what I meant," I say, recognizing dangerous territory. "Just that financial realities are different for everyone."

He holds my gaze for a moment longer, then nods. "You never know who's who in the zoo." He reaches into his backpack and pulls out several printed articles. "Sports psychology research. Thought these might help."

I take the papers, surprised by his preparation. Each article has sections highlighted, notes scrawled in the margins. "This is...thorough."

"Disappointed?" A hint of a smile plays on his lips. "Expected me to show up empty-handed so you could save the day?"

"Maybe," I lie, returning his almost-smile. I had *fully* expected him to show up empty-handed. "Though after yesterday's library ambush, I guess I shouldn't be surprised, huh?"

"Sorry, I hadn't meant to startle you." His words sound like a smirk even though his face remains earnest.

Something about him gives me the impression that he's on the inside of something in which I'm on the outside. I hate that. But I'm smarter than him; I'll figure it out.

"I think I was more surprised to see you in the *library* more than anything." I hope that didn't come out as smarmily as I intended.

"Fair enough," he says with that knowing smile, then steers us away from that topic: "What do you think of the research?"

We spend the next hour dissecting the articles, finding connections to the literary examples I've chosen. Despite my initial reservations, Branwen proves himself knowledgeable about sports psychology concepts, drawing parallels I wouldn't have considered.

"The fixation athletes develop on perfecting technique," he explains, leaning forward, "it's not that different from Heathcliff's obsession with Catherine. Both consume the individual. They distort reality."

"But athletic obsession can be channeled positively," I counter. "It has boundaries, rules."

"Does it?" His voice drops lower. "You ever watch a hockey game? I mean *really* watch? There are regulations and there are rules. Everyone's supposed to follow the regulations, but the best players make their own rules. They figure out how to exist in that gray space between control and chaos."

The way he says it—with a quiet intensity that borders on reverence—sends a shiver through me. For a moment, I glimpse something beneath his carefully maintained surface, a glimpse of passion that feels almost vulnerable.

"Is that where you exist?" I ask. "In the gray space?"

His eyes meet mine, startlingly direct. "Absolutely. Life's boring when everything's black and white."

The air feels suddenly charged and intimate in a way that has nothing to do with our academic discussion. I break the connection first, reaching for my coffee cup only to find it empty.

"I'll get you another," Branwen says, rising before I can protest. "Same thing?"

I nod, watching as he moves to the counter. The barista—Eliza, who works the same weekend shifts I do—smiles too widely at him, twirling her hair as she takes his order. I feel an unexpected pang of...something. Not jealousy. Definitely not that.

The café door opens again, admitting a group of students laughing and shaking the rain from their coats. Helena is in the group. Her blonde hair is perfectly styled despite the weather. Because of course it is. She spots me immediately, her smile thinning as she detaches from her friends.

"Tesni," she says, approaching my table. "Studying alone?"

"Actually—"

"She's with me." Branwen appears at Helena's shoulder, carrying two mugs. His voice is pleasant, but there's an edge to it that makes Helena's smile falter.

"Branwen," she says, recovering quickly. "I didn't realize you two were so close."

"Just project partners," I clarify, though the explanation feels inadequate under her scrutinizing gaze.

"How sweet." Her eyes flick between us. "I'm surprised Professor Hawthorne would pair you together, given the circumstances."

"Wait, what circumstances?" I ask before I can stop myself.

Helena's smile widens. "Oh, you don't know? I assumed Branwen would have mentioned his history with female project partners."

Branwen sets the mugs down. "Helena," he says, voice eerily calm. "Don't you have somewhere to be?"

She ignores him, leaning closer to me. "Ask him about Meredith Chen, from last semester's Sports Ethics class. Or don't they matter to you—the girls who came before?"

"Helena? I asked you really nicely." Branwen's voice has dropped to a dangerous register.

Helena goes from a jubilant-if-insincere queen bee to a withering flower in a millisecond. "Just looking out for a fellow student." She glances at our project notes. "Good luck with your...collaboration. Hope it ends better than the last one."

She saunters away, rejoining her friends at a table across the café. They huddle together, glancing our way with poorly disguised interest.

"What was that about?" I ask when I'm sure she's out of earshot.

Branwen sits down, his movements are carefully controlled. "Helena has a talent for twisting things."

"So, there's something to twist? Who's Meredith Chen?"

He meets my gaze, his expression guarded. "A project partner from last year. We had a disagreement about the direction of our work. She dropped the class. Helena's making it sound like something it wasn't. Some people just need drama, even when there isn't any."

His explanation is plausible, but it feels incomplete—curated, even. I think of Sophia's warnings, and the whispers that follow Branwen across campus. But I also remember how carefully he annotated those research articles and how he defended me against Helena just now.

"Okay," I say finally.

"Okay?" He looks surprised. "You believe me?"

"I *believe* that I will make my own judgments." I take a sip of the fresh coffee he brought. "Though it would be easier if people would stop being cryptic and just tell me what I'm supposed to be afraid of."

Something like respect flickers in his eyes. "Maybe they're trying to protect you."

"From what?"

He doesn't answer immediately, turning his mug slowly between his palms. "People see what they expect to see, Tesni. Once you get a certain reputation, everything you do gets filtered through it."

The vulnerability in his voice catches me off guard. For a moment, the mask slips, and I glimpse something raw beneath—hurt, maybe, or resignation. It tugs at something in me, that instinct my mother always warned would get me in trouble: the need to find the good in people, to believe in redemption.

"I know," I admit quietly. "When you're a scholarship kid, people assume things. That I don't belong. That I'm not smart enough to be here on merit."

"But you are," he says with surprising conviction. "You're the only one in Professor Hawthorne's class with anything to say that didn't come straight from the Internet."

The compliment warms me more than it should. "How would you know? You just started."

A hesitation, barely perceptible. "I've heard you. Before. In the dining hall, talking to Sophia about books. You get...animated. It's noticeable. Small campus, right?"

The idea that he's been watching me, listening to me, before we even met should be creepy at worst and unsettling at best. Instead, I'm oddly flattered, even though part of me knows that I should know better.

We work for another hour, the conversation flowing more easily now. Branwen has a sharp mind beneath his brooding exterior, catching nuances in the texts I've highlighted that even I missed. As we gather our things to leave, the rain has stopped, leaving the streets gleaming under the streetlights.

"I'll walk you back," Branwen says, slinging his bag over his shoulder.

"I'm headed to the library, actually. Still have reading to do."

"Then I'll walk you there."

His insistence should annoy me, but after Helena's hostility, his protective presence feels like a warm blanket. We walk in comfortable silence, the campus quiet in the early evening. Fallen leaves stick to the wet pavement, creating a patchwork of amber and crimson.

"When's your next game?" I ask as we approach the library's imposing facade.

"Saturday. Against EC Thornfield." Something hard enters his voice. "You should come."

"I don't even know the rules."

"You don't need to." He stops at the library steps, looking down at me. "Think of it as research for the project: you get to see the obsession in action."

"For the project," I repeat, not quite believing that's his motivation for inviting me but unable to glean any other feasible reason. "Maybe I will."

He nods, seemingly satisfied. "Text me when you're done here. I don't like the idea of you walking back alone."

"I do it all the time."

"That doesn't make it smart. Text me." His tone leaves no room for argument.

"Fine," I concede, though part of me bristles at being told what to do. "Thanks for the work session. And the coffee."

"Anytime." He hesitates, then adds, "Don't believe everything you hear. About me or anyone else. This place runs on rumors, and there's two sides to every story."

With that, he turns and walks away and his figure is soon swallowed by the evening shadows before I can broach further.

Inside the library, I find a quiet corner and spread out my books. But concentration eludes me, my thoughts circling back to Branwen, to Helena's insinuations, and to the vulnerability beneath his guarded exterior. I'm so distracted that I nearly miss the small white envelope tucked between the pages of my textbook.

I open it, expecting a library notice or perhaps a note from Sophia. Instead, I find a single sheet of paper with words cut from what looks like magazine pages, pasted in an uneven line:

STAY AWAY FROM HIM IF YOU KNOW WHAT'S GOOD FOR YOU

No signature. And, no explanation needed—the "him" can only be Branwen.

I should be alarmed, maybe even scared. Instead, I feel a surge of indignation. Who does Helena—because who else could it be?—think she is, trying to intimidate me with childish threats?

Though I do feel like a child—who wants to do exactly what someone is telling me to avoid.

I crumple the note and toss it into my bag, determined to ignore it. Just a petty attempt to rattle me. But as I try to return to my reading, the words keep flashing in my mind, along with Helena's smirking face and Branwen's warning: *Don't believe everything you hear.*

The question is, what should I believe? The rumors, the warnings, the threatening note? Or the glimpses of something more complex I've seen lurking beneath Branwen Atthill's ice-blue eyes?

I feel my phone vibrate and see a text:

Made it to the library safely?

The concern in those simple words shouldn't affect me so strongly. I type back a quick *Yes, all good* before returning to my books, trying to ignore the warmth spreading through my chest and the nagging voice that sounds suspiciously like Sophia's, whispering that I might be making a terrible mistake.

6

Dangerous Liaisons

Branwen

The puck slides across the ice, a perfect pass. I don't take it. My eyes are fixed on Gardner, EC Thornfield's star forward, who's been running his mouth since the first period. Behind me, Jenkins shouts something, but his voice is just noise. Everything narrows to a single point: Gardner's smug face as he intercepts the pass meant for me.

Focus, Atthill.

I surge forward, blades cutting deep, the burn in my thighs barely registering. Gardner thinks he's fast. He's not. I catch him at the blue line, driving my shoulder into his chest harder than necessary. He goes down, skidding across the ice. The crowd roars—half cheers, half boos.

The whistle blares. Penalty.

Coach Hendricks' face is purple as I skate to the box. Two minutes for charging. Worth it to see Gardner spit blood onto the ice.

"What the hell was that?" Jenkins yells as I pass him.

I ignore him, dropping onto the bench in the penalty box. My heartbeat pounds in my ears, drowning out the crowd's noise. Across the arena, I scan the stands automatically—searching, always searching. And there she is, five rows up, wearing a UC Wisteria scarf. Tesni. She came.

Something shifts in my chest, a tightness I hadn't noticed until it eased. My focus sharpens, clarity returning like ice water in my veins. She's watching. Every move I make now matters more.

When I return to the ice, I'm transformed. The next twenty minutes are perfect hockey—controlled aggression, precise passes, and a beautiful goal that puts us ahead in the third period. Coach nods grimly from the bench, as close to approval as he gets. The final buzzer sounds with UC Wisteria up 3-2.

In the locker room, the team celebrates around me. Milo cranks *Afterlife* on his speaker, bass thrumming through the concrete floor. Jenkins claps my shoulder as he passes, our earlier tension forgotten in the glow of victory.

"Good game, Atthill," he says. "When you're not busy trying to murder someone."

I force a smile, the expression feeling foreign on my face. "Gotta keep it interesting."

He laughs, moving on to congratulate the freshman goalie. I shower quickly, eager to get out of here. My phone has three new messages, all from her:

Great goal!

I think I'm starting to understand hockey. Maybe.

Still at the arena, is there somewhere teams meet after games?

My pulse quickens. She's waiting for me. I dress faster than I ever have, ignoring Hendricks' request for a post-game talk. Nothing matters except getting to her before she leaves, before someone else does.

I find her in the lobby, looking small and uncertain amidst groups of rowdy fans. She's shivering slightly, even with the scarf around her neck. When she spots me, her face lights up in a way that sends a jolt straight through me.

"You came," I say.

"For research," she replies with a small smile. "Though I didn't expect it to be so...violent."

"That was nothing." I step closer, drawn to her warmth. "You should see when we really hate the other team."

"Do you hate EC Thornfield?"

I hate everyone who isn't you.

"Professional rivalry," I say. "I have some...history with their captain."

She nods, accepting this without pressing further. It's one of the things I'm growing to appreciate about her. She doesn't dig unnecessarily and doesn't demand explanations for things that don't concern her.

"You played well," she says. "At least, the crowd seemed to think so?"

"I played better after I saw you in the stands."

Her cheeks flush, and the color is beautiful on her pale skin. "I doubt that had anything to do with it."

"It did." I reach for her hand, an impulse I don't try to control. She lets me, and her fingers are cold against mine. "Let me buy you dinner. To thank you for coming."

She hesitates, and I can see her weighing it—Sophia's warnings probably echo in her head; maybe Helena's, too. But then she nods. "Dinner sounds good."

Triumph surges through me. I guide her through the crowd, my hand at the small of her back, glaring at anyone who comes too close. Outside, the night air is crisp with impending winter, and the campus is quiet except for distant celebration sounds from the direction of Greek Row.

"Where are we going?" she asks as we walk.

"There's a diner just off campus. Best burgers in town." I steer her toward University Avenue, hyperaware of how close she is and how she matches her stride to mine.

"Atthill!" The voice cuts through the night. Coach Hendricks strides toward us, face set in hard lines. "A word."

Tesni glances between us. "I can wait over there." She points to a nearby bench.

"No need," I tell her, then to Hendricks, "I'm kind of in the middle of something. Can it wait?"

"It can't." His tone leaves no room for argument. He nods to Tesni. "Miss, would you excuse us for a moment?"

She steps away reluctantly, moving to the bench. I watch her go, irritation burning in my chest.

"What?" I demand when she's out of earshot.

Hendricks' eyes narrow. "You skipped mandatory practice yesterday. Then today, you nearly take Gardner's head off in the first period before deciding to actually play hockey in the third. What's going on with you?"

"What were *you* watching? Because from where I was standing, I won the fucking game for us."

"That's not the point, and you know it." He lowers his voice. "I've been coaching for twenty years. I know when a player's got off-ice issues affecting his game. Whatever's going on with you, fix it."

"Nothing's going on." The lie comes easily.

Hendricks' gaze shifts to Tesni, waiting patiently on the bench. "That her? The one Jenkins mentioned?"

My hands curl into fists at my sides. Jenkins. That nosy bastard. "Jenkins just wants to cause problems."

"Listen to me carefully, son." Hendricks steps closer, voice dropping further. "I covered for you last year with the Davis incident. Said what the university wanted to hear. But I'm watching you now, and I don't like what I see. Get your head straight, or I'll bench you for the season. Scholarship or not."

The threat hangs in the air between us. I force myself to relax my hands and keep my expression neutral. "Understood, Coach."

He holds my gaze a moment longer, then nods curtly. "See that you do." With a final glance at Tesni, he turns and walks away.

I stand motionless, breathing deeply to control the rage bubbling beneath the surface. How dare he threaten me? How dare Jenkins talk about Tesni? The urge to follow Hendricks, to make him understand exactly who he's dealing with, is nearly overwhelming.

But then I feel a gentle touch on my arm, and the anger recedes like a wave pulling back from the shore.

"Everything okay?" Tesni asks. She looks concerned.

I look down at her hand on my arm, marveling at how such a slight touch can anchor me. "Yeah. Just hockey stuff."

"He seemed upset."

"He's always upset." I place my hand over hers, keeping it against my arm as we resume walking.

She doesn't pull away, and the small victory makes me generous. "Tell me about your week," I say as we approach the diner. Its neon sign casts blue and pink light across her face.

She tenses slightly, and I know she's about to hold something back.

"Same as usual," she says unconvincingly.

I watch her unwrap her scarf, exposing the delicate line of her neck. Three weeks since our first project meeting, and I've cataloged a hundred such details: the constellation of freckles on her left wrist, the way she tucks her hair behind her ear when concentrating, how she bites her lower lip when she's choosing her words carefully.

"You can trust me," I say. "Seriously. If anyone knows about a weight on their shoulder, it's me. Talk to me."

I can see the wheels in her head, deliberating. This moment feels...big. When she trusts me with something important or decides she needs to wait further.

"I got a weird note."

"A note? Like, between recess and study hall?" I smile, but she does not. Whatever she's talking about, it's clearly nothing funny. "What happened? What kind of note?"

She sighs. "About you, actually. Saying I should stay away from you."

"Have you told anyone?"

"I'm telling you, aren't I?" She smiles, but there's a hint of strain behind it. "Besides, it would take more than some cut-and-paste note to scare me off."

"Off what?"

She pauses. "The project. Our partnership."

Our partnership. Such an inadequate term for what's growing between us. She doesn't see it yet, but she will.

The waitress interrupts to take our orders. Tesni asks for a chocolate shake and fries, and the simple, childlike order makes something twist in my chest. I order a burger and coffee, though food is the last thing on my mind.

"So," she says when the waitress leaves, "I've been thinking about our project. What if we narrow our focus to obsession as a form of identity creation? In literature, characters like Heathcliff define themselves through their obsession with another person. In sports, athletes often construct their identity around competitive excellence."

I lean forward, drawing her into academic discussion, the safe space where she's most comfortable with me. "Not just excellence. Domination. It's about power; having it, keeping it, using it."

"Is that how you see hockey? As domination?"

The question is innocent, but it stirs something darker. "I see everything that way," I admit, watching her reaction carefully. "The world runs on power dynamics, Tesni. Who has control, who doesn't. Who takes, who gives."

She considers this, head tilted slightly. "That's a bleak view."

"Is it?" I reach across the table, my fingers brushing hers. "What about you? What power dynamics are you caught in?"

The question startles her. "I don't think of life that way."

"Doesn't make it any less real. The scholarship student navigating elite academia? The small-town girl at the big university? None of that feels like a power struggle?"

Her eyes widen slightly, and I know I've touched something real. "Sometimes," she admits quietly. "It's exhausting. I always feel like I have to prove I belong."

"You don't have to prove anything to me."

Our food arrives, breaking the moment. She dips a fry in her shake. It's odd and inexplicably endearing. I watch her eat while barely touching my own food, content to observe.

"We should adjust our meeting schedule," I say casually. "With midterms coming up, the library's going to be packed."

"What did you have in mind?"

"My place. It's quiet, no distractions. We could get more done."

She hesitates, warning flags clearly going up. "I don't know..."

"Or yours," I offer, though the thought of her tiny dorm room with her roommate and constant interruptions is far from ideal. But I can't push too hard; not yet. "I'm flexible."

"Maybe we could try the study rooms in the athletic center?" she suggests. "I've heard they're usually empty in the evenings."

Not what I wanted, but it's a step closer—more private than the library, a space where I have some influence. "That works. I can book us the corner room. It has the best view of campus."

She smiles and relaxes her shoulders. "Perfect. How about tomorrow night? I have a paper due Monday that I need to finish, but I'm free after eight."

"Eight it is." I pull out my phone, making a show of checking my calendar. "Actually, I have an idea. The athletics department has a sports psychology session at seven. Guest lecturer from ECU talking about performance anxiety and obsessive training patterns. Might be perfect research for our project."

Her eyes light up with academic interest, exactly as I knew they would. "That does sound relevant. But would I be allowed in? I'm not an athlete."

"You'd be with me," I say as if that settles everything. And it does because after only a brief hesitation, she nods.

"Okay. The lecture, then study room after."

Victory tastes sweet. I hide my satisfaction behind a sip of coffee, already planning tomorrow's careful choreography. The lecture is real; I didn't need to invent that, but I didn't tell her that it's in the restricted section of the athletic center, far from the main campus, in a building where few students venture after dark. I'll book the study room at the end of a deserted hallway, soundproofed for "athletes' concentration."

The academic discussion seems to organically get more...personal. She talks about her childhood, which sounds pretty rough. Single mother who worked two jobs just to keep the lights on and was rarely home; dad who bounced when she was five and never so much as wrote her a Christmas card.

Then she talks about books, how she found solace in them and felt less alone. She doesn't say it overtly, but I get the sense that she's felt very alone for a long time. And I don't say it, but I'm going to change that. She's never going to feel alone again.

Whenever she tries to steer the convo back to me, I give her carefully curated details of my own past—enough to seem like I'm being open (my dad's abusive tendencies, the pressures of high-level hockey) without revealing the uglier truths.

As we walk back toward campus, the night has grown colder. Tesni shivers beside me, and I seize the opportunity to put my arm around her shoulders. She stiffens momentarily, then relaxes against me.

"Thanks for coming to the game," I say as we approach her dormitory. "It meant a lot."

"I enjoyed it more than I thought I would," she says. "I still don't understand all the rules, though."

"Next time, I'll explain everything." Next time. The promise of continuity, of future moments together, feels significant.

We stop at the entrance to her building, suddenly feeling a little awkward. This is the part where I should say goodnight, should let her go inside, should be satisfied with the progress I've made today.

I can't do it.

"Tesni," I say. "I need to know something."

She looks up at me, eyes wide and questioning in the dim light. "What?"

"Those notes. The warnings about me. Do they scare you?"

Her answer matters more than it should. I hold my breath, waiting.

"No," she says finally. "They make me curious."

Relief floods through me, followed immediately by a darker satisfaction. Curious. It's enough for now. More than enough.

"Good," I murmur, reaching out to tuck a strand of hair behind her ear. My fingers linger against her cheek. "I'm not what they say I am. But I'm not what you think either."

Confusion flickers across her face. "What does that mean?"

"It means be careful what you wish to know about people." I step back and let my hand drop before I can do something I'll regret. Not yet. Not here. "Goodnight, Tesni. I'll see you tomorrow at seven."

I walk away without waiting for her response, feeling her eyes on my back. The night air does nothing to cool the heat beneath my skin; the burning needs that grow stronger each time I'm with her.

Back in my apartment, I check the team Insta account, which posts photos of everyone from the game—including the fans—and find one with her. I zoom in, crop out the people on either side, and run it through a filter. After sending it to my laptop and hitting print, I add the photo to my wall—her, at the hockey game, scarf around her neck, eyes following my movement on the ice.

Beneath it, I've begun mapping our interactions on a timeline, noting each point of progress: first conversation, first coffee, first touch. Tomorrow will bring new milestones.

My phone buzzes with a text from her:

Thanks for dinner. Looking forward to the lecture tomorrow.

I stare at the message, at the casual politeness that reveals nothing of what she's really thinking. Is she lying in bed now, replaying our conversation? Wondering about my cryptic parting words? I close my eyes, imagining her in her tiny dorm room, thinking of me.

Another text arrives, this one from Jenkins:

Coach asked about you and that scholarship girl. Told him you're just project partners. Was I lying?

The intrusion of his name on my screen, connected to Tesni's, sends a surge of rage through me. I hurl the phone across the room, where it hits the wall and clatters to the floor. The sound is unsatisfying. I need to break something bigger that shatters with more verve; I need to feel the release that only destruction brings.

I grab a glass from the sink and smash it against the counter, relishing the sharp crack, the spray of fragments across the linoleum. Better, but not enough.

I sink to the floor, back against the wall, and force myself to breathe deeply. To think. Tesni wouldn't want this. She definitely wouldn't understand this part of me—not yet, at least. I have to manage this aspect of myself with caution until she's ready to see all of me.

When my heartbeat slows, I retrieve my phone; the screen protector saved it from any real damage. I don't reply to Jenkins—that asshole can sit and wonder—and check my calendar instead, confirming tomorrow's schedule. The lecture. The study room. The carefully orchestrated opportunities to draw her closer.

Seven hours before I see her again. Seven hours to master the storm inside me, to prepare the version of myself she needs to see.

I cross to the bathroom and open the medicine cabinet, reaching for the small orange bottle tucked behind the aspirin. The pills inside are my compromise with control—prescribed at the hospital after the Davis fight, meant to be tolerated and then abandoned after I was back to myself on the ice.

But tonight, I need to feel and silence the darkest impulses that threaten to surface when I think about Jenkins asking questions, about Hendricks making threats, about anyone trying to come between me and what's mine.

One white pill dissolves on my tongue. I stare at my reflection in the mirror; it's a stranger I barely recognize. Oxy does weird things to people. Sometimes, before you escape reality, you get sped up; that's what happens to me, anyway. But this isn't who Tesni sees. It definitely isn't who she's drawn to.

"Control," I whisper to my reflection. "Just a little longer."

Tomorrow, I'll take another step in bringing her into my world. Each meeting is carefully planned, and each interaction is designed to tighten the connection between us. The study room after will provide comfort, privacy, and an opportunity to position myself as her protector. Which, after all, is what she needs. She already told me how lonely life has been, and her scumbag dad left her without a strong man to look after her. That's what she needs.

I return to the main room and stand before the wall of photos, reaching out to trace the outline of her face in the newest addition. "Soon," I promise her. "Soon you'll understand we're meant to be together. That no one else sees you like I do. That no one else ever will."

The pill begins to take effect, smoothing the jagged edges of my thoughts. I lie on my bed, still fully clothed, and stare at the ceiling. Seven hours. I can wait. I've gotten good at waiting, at planning, at taking exactly what I want in precisely the right moment.

And what I want is Tesni Solaris—her light, her warmth, her innocence. All of it, mine to possess. Mine to consume.

Mine to keep.

7

Temptation and Tension

Tesni

Unlike the ivy-draped buildings at the heart of campus, the athletic center is all glass and steel, modern and intimidating. I check my phone—6:55 PM. Branwen should be waiting inside.

I hesitate at the entrance. The past week has been a blur, and each interaction with Branwen has been more intense than the last. His focus on me is almost overwhelming—the way he tracks my movements, how he seems to materialize whenever I'm alone, and his uncanny knowledge of my schedule. It should disturb me. But it makes me feel something I haven't felt in a long time...safe.

The door swings open before I can reach for it. Branwen stands there as if he's been watching for me. He's dressed in athletic pants and a fitted UC Wisteria quarter-zip that emphasizes the breadth of his shoulders.

"Wasn't sure you'd show," he says.

"I always do what I say I will." His reaction to that is strange, almost as if he wants to edit that sentence, but I don't press. I step inside.

His hand finds the small of my back, guiding me through the lobby. "Lecture's in the performance psychology wing. This way."

The athletic center is a maze of corridors and specialized facilities. We pass a state-of-the-art weight room, an Olympic-sized pool glowing ethereal blue, and rehabilitation rooms with equipment I don't recognize.

"People actually study here?" I ask, unable to keep the awe from my voice.

Branwen's lips curve into an almost-smile. "Athletic scholarships come with perks. One of the few advantages of being university property."

There's an edge to his words. "Is that how you see yourself? As property?"

His eyes meet mine, surprisingly vulnerable. "Pretty much. Whatever they give, they can take away just as quickly. It's all about their bottom line. Are you worth what they're shelling out for you to go here?"

It's both a question he's asking as a general principle, but it feels directed at me, too, as if to show that he understands what it's like for me. And, even though he's on an athletic scholarship, I guess we're both the university's property.

The bitterness in his tone stirs something protective in me. Before I can respond, we turn down a corridor that's darker than the others.

"It's through here," he says, stopping at a door marked "Performance Psychology Suite." He pushes the door open.

The room beyond is smaller than I expected. It's arranged like a seminar space, with about thirty chairs facing a podium. Most seats are already filled. Some of them turn as we enter.

"Atthill," one of them calls—a massive guy with a wrestler's build. "Didn't expect to see you at one of these voluntary sessions."

"Broadening my horizons, Martinez," Branwen replies coolly. His hand, still resting on my back, presses slightly firmer.

Martinez's gaze shifts to me, and he smirks. "I bet you are."

Branwen's posture stiffens, but before he can respond, a slender woman in a tailored suit approaches the podium. "Let's begin," she announces.

We take seats in the back row. The space between our chairs is minimal, and Branwen's knee presses against mine as he settles in. I don't move away.

The lecturer introduces herself as Dr. Eleanor Vance from Eastern College University, a specialist in athletic psychology with a focus on obsessive training patterns. Her presentation is fascinating—exploring the line between productive dedication and destructive fixation, illustrated with case studies of athletes whose intense focus both elevated and ultimately derailed their careers.

"The most elite athletes," she explains, showing a slide of Olympic medalists, "often exist in a liminal space between obsession and discipline. They channel potentially destructive impulses into structured achievement."

Branwen leans forward, completely absorbed. I study his profile in the dim light—the sharp jaw, the intensity in his eyes. Is that what he does? Channel darker impulses into the structured violence of hockey?

"However," Dr. Vance continues, "when the structure fails, or when life events trigger underlying psychological vulnerabilities, this same focus can become dangerous—to the athlete and others."

The next slide shows newspaper headlines: *Star Athlete Arrested After Stalking Ex-Girlfriend, Olympic Hopeful's Career Ends After Violent Outburst, The Thin Line Between Dedication and Delusion.*

A chill runs through me. Branwen's hand suddenly covers mine, his fingers intertwining with my own. The gesture feels possessive, almost desperate. When I look at him, his eyes are fixed on the headlines and there's something unreadable in his expression.

"You okay?" I whisper.

He blinks, almost as if returns to himself. "Fine," he murmurs but doesn't release my hand.

There are so many words on that slide that should scare me. *Stalking. Outburst. Delusion.* He plays one of the most violent sports on the planet and if even half the rumors about him are true, he'd be a likely candidate for any of those behaviors.

But I keep my hand entombed in his, leaning against his shoulder even while my heart does gymnastics in my chest, as if telling my brain to use itself.

In this moment, there's a disconnect that I can't explain. I can only lean into it or lean away, and I choose the former. I feel my body shiver, and I know he can feel the same. We both know it's not because of the cold. But neither one of us addresses it.

The lecture continues for another forty minutes, delving into intervention strategies and psychological safeguards. Throughout, Branwen's hold remains firm, his thumb occasionally tracing circles on my skin in a way that makes concentration increasingly difficult.

When it ends, there's a smattering of applause. Athletes rise, some approaching Dr. Vance with questions, others filtering out in small groups. Branwen stands, pulling me gently with him.

"What did you think?" he asks as we exit.

"It was illuminating," I reply honestly. "Especially her points about the relationship between childhood trauma and fixation patterns in elite athletes."

Something flickers in his eyes. "You caught that."

"Of course. It's relevant to our project, isn't it? The parallel between traumatic origins creating obsessive personalities in both literature and sports."

He studies me for a moment, then nods. "The study room's this way."

We move deeper into the building, leaving the populated areas behind.

"Are you sure this is open to students?" I ask, noticing the card readers beside each entrance.

"Some," he says, stopping at a door at the end of the corridor.

The room he unlocks is more like a private lounge—comfortable seating, a large table, and a small kitchenette in one corner. Floor-to-ceiling windows offer a panoramic view of the campus below, now lit by streetlights.

"Wow," I breathe, moving to the windows. "You weren't kidding about the view."

Branwen closes the door behind us. The soft click of the lock engaging seems unusually loud in the quiet room. "Athletics department spares no expense for their assets," he says, that bitter edge returning.

I turn to face him. "It must be...strange, no? Being valued for what you do rather than who you are?"

He looks surprised. "Most people just see the perks and special treatment."

"You should know by now that I'm not most people."

"No," he says, stepping closer, that same look resurfacing in all its obnoxiously charming confidence—the one that implies he knows something I don't; this time, it's as if he knows more about me than I do. "No, you're not."

There's an intensity to the moment that makes my heart race. I move to the table, setting down my bag. "We should probably get to work."

He follows, dropping into the chair next to mine. "Always so focused. What drives you, Tesni? What are you chasing with all this academic perfection?"

The question catches me off guard. "I'm not chasing anything; I'm trying to keep my scholarship. They kick me out if I don't maintain a high enough GPA."

"It's more than that." His eyes search mine. "I've seen how you push yourself. You could hit their GPA minimum in your sleep. It's something more."

I look away, uncomfortable with his perception. "I told you, my mom sacrificed everything to get me here. I can't waste that."

"And what about what *you* want? Beyond obligation, beyond proving yourself—what does Tesni Solaris desire?"

The question hangs between us, strangely intimate. "To be seen for who I really am."

Something shifts in his expression, a hunger that should alarm me but doesn't. "I see you," he says, voice low. "Better than anyone else."

I shiver slightly. I don't know what's worse, that he thinks that or that I believe he might be right. This guy hardly knows me, has hardly spent enough time with me to really see me; but maybe all it comes down to is whether someone wants to see you—and he does.

"Tell me about your mother," he says suddenly.

I blink at the shift. "Why?"

"Because she shaped you. Because I want to know everything about you." The naked honesty in his voice disarms me.

"We had a one-bedroom above a laundromat. It was in a part of town where the laundromats were called *lavanderias*, if that tells you anything. Not the kind of place you'd want to go walking alone at night. But I always had a new book; and the time I did get to spend with her, I cherished it so much."

"You guys still close?"

"We're both drinking from the firehose, but as close as we can be, yeah. I just want to make her proud, you know? Make her sacrifices...mean something."

"I'm sure she brags about you all the time. She sounds amazing. Just like you."

I think I squeak out a "thank you," but I'm too concerned about my face showing how I'm feeling—understood; seen; appreciated.

"What about your parents?" I ask, realizing how little I know about him beyond the fact that his dad wasn't much of one.

His expression darkens. "Not much to tell. My dad was the stereotypical drunk who went to get cigarettes when I was nine and never came home. Guess he'd run out of new and exciting ways to kick the shit out of me. Mom checked out long before that—physically present but mentally, not so much."

"I'm sorry," I say softly, resisting the urge to touch him.

He shrugs. "Made me self-sufficient. Taught me early that people leave, that nothing lasts. Useful lesson."

The pain he's trying to hide is so raw, so familiar to anyone who's ever felt abandoned, that my heart constricts. I suspect this is the source of his intensity and need for control.

"Not everyone leaves," I say, unable to stop myself from reaching for his hand.

He stares at our joined fingers. "You will. Eventually. When you see what I really am."

"And what's that?"

"In the army, they call it 'FUBAR'. Fucked Up Beyond All Recognition. Just to say, I'm long past the point of fixing."

"I don't believe that—of you or anyone."

A harsh laugh escapes him. "You sound like Dr. Vance with her intervention strategies. Some people can't be fixed, Tesni."

"Or maybe they just haven't found the right reason to try." I lean closer.

Something shifts in his expression. "And you think I've found that reason?" The way he says it, each word sounds like a wink.

"I think everyone deserves a chance to be more than their past," I say.

He studies me, then releases my hand abruptly. "We should work on the project."

The suddenness of it leaves me disoriented. I dig through my bag for my notes, trying to focus back on studying. "Right. I was thinking we could structure the thesis around three main parallels—"

"Why did you really come tonight?" He cuts in.

I blink at him, startled by his directness. "For the project. For research."

"Bullshit." The word isn't harsh, just matter-of-fact. "You knew it was isolated. You knew what Sophia would say. What everyone would say about you being alone with me."

Heat creeps up my cheeks. "I'm capable of making my own decisions."

"But why this one?" He leans closer, his gaze unwavering. "Tell me the truth, Tesni."

The truth is more complicated than I want to admit, even to myself. I'm drawn to him. I like how he looks at me like I'm the only person in the world who matters. It's intoxicating to be the center of someone's universe, especially when I've spent so much of my life feeling invisible.

"Because," I begin, then trail off. I try again. "Because I'm curious about you. Because when you talk, I want to listen. Because—"

The library is too still, just the faint hum of the vents. Somewhere deeper in the stacks a phone speaker leaked Jutes's "Sleepyhead," the chorus drifting like a half-dream.

His movement is unexpected. One moment we're talking, the next his hand grips my wrist, firm but not painful, and he pulls me toward him. Before I can react, his lips crash against mine, hungry and demanding.

I freeze, caught between shock and a rush of sensation. His kiss isn't gentle—it's possessive, almost desperate as if he's been holding back for too long. His free hand tangles in my hair, holding me in place.

Everything feels way out of my control, which should scare me, but doesn't; I don't know what to make of that. I remember an old teacher saying that animals grow to love their cages. That's how I feel; encaged but enraptured.

It feels like I'm in fight or flight mode but unsure which action achieves which outcome—and what outcome I *really* want to achieve.

Because all the common sense accumulated in my brain tells me to push him away, yell for help, do *something* to make him cede control.

But I don't want him to.

No one has kissed me like this before—this is raw, primal, consuming.

When he finally pulls back, his breathing is ragged, his eyes darkened with want. His grip on my wrist remains firm, as if he's afraid I'll flee. "Tell me to stop," he says, voice rough. "Tell me this isn't what you want."

This is so messed up. And amazing. I thought I'd felt everything, but never this—someone who can see through defenses and coping mechanisms and into my soul. A guy who knows me so well, I can't even imagine how well he'd know my contours...

But I can't. Because despite the warnings and the red flags, I do want this. Want *him*. Want to be the one who reaches the heart no one else can touch, who heals what others have broken.

"I don't want you to stop," I whisper.

Something flashes in his eyes before he pulls me to him again. This kiss is different, deeper, his tongue sliding against mine in a way that draws an involuntary sound from my throat. His hands roam now, one still tangled in my hair, the other sliding down my back to press me closer.

Time loses meaning as we lose ourselves in each other. I'm vaguely aware of movement, of being guided backward until I'm pressed against the window, the coolness of the glass a pleasant contrast to the warmth that's built up inside me...

I take off his shirt. His abs are out of an Abercrombie catalog, and his arms are veiny and bulging with sinewy strength.

It feels like that liminal space between reality and dream; I'm both in control of my body and watching myself from afar, giving him dominion over every part of me.

"Tesni," he murmurs against my throat, my name a reverence and a claim. "You have no idea how long I've wanted this. Wanted you."

We've known each other barely a month, but this is a passion like in the novels I've devoured, all-consuming and immediate. This is being truly wanted, truly seen.

His hand slides beneath the hem of my sweater, warm against my bare skin. The touch brings a jolt of reality and I snap out of my reverie, the logical part of my brain coming awake after a period of dormancy. "Branwen," I gasp, placing my hand over his. "Wait."

To my surprise, he stills instantly, though his breathing remains heavy, his eyes wild. "Too much?"

The concern in his voice touches something in me. This powerful, intimidating man pauses at my slightest hesitation.

"Not too much," I assure him. "Just...fast."

He releases me slowly, reluctantly, though he doesn't step away. "I scared you."

"No," I say, and it's mostly true. What scares me isn't his intensity but my response to it—how readily I surrendered to his touch, how much I wanted more. "I just need to catch my breath."

He reaches up, tucking a strand of hair behind my ear. "You're trembling."

I am, though not from fear. "It's a lot to process."

His thumb traces my lower lip. "Regrets already?"

"No," I say. "Just...what is this, Branwen? What are we doing?"

His expression hardens slightly. "What do you want it to be?"

The question feels like a test, though I'm not sure of what. I opt for honesty: "I don't know. But I know I want to find out."

His posture relaxes slightly, and he steps back, giving me space. "Good. Because I'm not letting you go, Tesni. Not now that I know you feel this too."

The possessiveness sends a thrill of excitement down my spine. No one has ever wanted me so fiercely before.

"We should probably actually work on the project," I say, attempting to steer us back to safer ground. "At least for a little while."

He smiles, slipping on his shirt. "Always the responsible one." He touches my cheek briefly. "It's one of the things I lo—like about you."

The near-slip hangs between us, neither of us acknowledging it. We spread out our notes, though concentration proves impossible with him sitting so close, his knee pressed against mine, his hand occasionally brushing mine as we work.

After an hour of minimal progress, I check my watch. "It's getting late. I should probably head back."

"I'll walk you," he says immediately, already gathering our things.

"You don't have to—"

"I do." His tone brooks no argument. "It's not safe for you to walk alone at night."

Part of me wants to assert my independence, to remind him I've been navigating campus after dark since freshman year. But another part—the part still buzzing from his kisses—is touched by his protectiveness.

We walk across campus in comfortable silence, his arm around my shoulders, warm against the night chill. The campus is quiet; most students already returned to dorms or departed for weekend activities.

"You were right," I tell him.

"About?"

"Why I came tonight. It wasn't just for the project."

He stops walking, turning to face me under the soft glow of a lamp post, his eyes widening as if he knows the answer but just wants to hear me say it. "No? Why, then?"

"Because when I'm with you, I feel...alive. Like there's more to the world than textbooks and grades. Like there's more to *me*."

His expression softens. "There's a lot more to you; more than you give yourself credit for. And it's time someone made you see that."

The sincerity in his voice touches something deep inside me. This is what I've always wanted—to matter enough to someone that they would put me, my needs, my desires, above their own.

"You already are," I tell him, rising on tiptoes to press a gentle kiss to his lips.

He responds with restraint, his hands light on my waist. When I pull back, his eyes remain closed for a moment.

"I should go," I whisper, though my body remains still.

"Text me when you're inside," he says, releasing me. "So I know you're safe."

I nod, stepping away. "Goodnight, Branwen."

"Sweet dreams." He remains rooted in place, watching as I walk toward my building.

As soon as he said "dreams," I knew that I would see him there tonight.

At the entrance, I turn back. He's still there, a solitary figure beneath the lamplight. Something about the image—his stillness, his patient vigilance—sends a shiver of both warmth and unease through me.

I lean against the closed door in my dorm room, heart racing. Sophia's warnings echo in my mind, but they're drowned out by the memory of Branwen's touch, his vulnerability when he spoke of his parents, and the way he looked at me like I was something precious and rare. Something worth protecting.

Everyone's wrong about him. He just needs someone to believe in him, to see past the reputation and the rough exterior. And I'm exactly the person to do that.

I send him a text:

Safely inside. Thank you for tonight.

His response comes immediately:

Dream of me. I'll be dreaming of you.

I curl up in bed, clutching my phone, smiling to myself despite the small voice of caution whispering in the back of my mind. Because that voice is no match for the intoxicating possibility that maybe I've found my epic love story after all.

8

Silent Stalker

Branwen

She's late.

I check my watch again—3:17 PM. Tesni's Victorian Lit class ended seventeen minutes ago. She should be crossing the quad by now, heading to the library for her Thursday study session. But she's nowhere to be found.

My fingers tap against the bench where I've been waiting, positioned between buildings with a clear view of her route. Students flow past, wrapped in coats against the November chill, none of them Tesni.

Something's wrong.

I pull out my phone, checking for messages and finding none. Anxiety crawls up my spine; it gets worse when I can't see her. We've been officially together for two weeks now, since that night in the study room. Two weeks of stolen kisses between classes, secret meetings in my apartment, and her gradual surrender to what's growing between us.

Two weeks of watching her more closely than ever.

Relief floods through me when I finally spot her, immediately followed by tension when I see she's not alone. Professor Hawthorne walks with her, leaning in too close as they talk. I can't hear them, but I can see the expression on her face and how she gestures when she's excited about something.

I feel my teeth grinding. Professor Hawthorne's interest in her has been obvious from the start, but lately, he's been inserting himself more frequently. Which is no good, but not quite reaching the level of a threat; not yet, at least.

I stand, moving toward the path they'll take. Not directly, but close enough to intercept naturally, as if by coincidence.

"...consider submitting it to the undergraduate journal," Professor Hawthorne is saying as they approach. "Your analysis is exceptionally insightful."

Tesni smiles, that bright, genuine expression that first caught me. "Thank you, Professor, but I think it needs more work before—"

"Tesni." I step into their path, my voice cutting through her response. "I've been looking for you."

Her eyes turn to half-dollars. "Branwen! I didn't expect to see you until tonight."

Professor Hawthorne's face reveals nothing, but I catch the subtle stiffening of his posture. "Mr. Atthill," he says evenly. "How's the joint project coming along?"

"Excellently," I reply, moving to Tesni's side, my arm sliding around her waist. "We've discovered we...complement each other really well."

A flash of disapproval crosses his angular face before it's quickly masked. "I'm pleased to hear it." He turns to Tesni. "Think about what I said. My office door is always open."

The double meaning isn't lost on me. My hand tightens slightly on Tesni's waist.

"Thank you, Professor," she says, seemingly oblivious. "I appreciate it."

I need to get this naivete out of her. It's adorable until it turns into letting others in.

Professor Hawthorne nods, eyes flicking to my possessive hold on her before he leaves. I watch him go. Another obstacle, if not threat. To be determined.

"Everything okay?" Tesni asks, bringing my attention back to her. "You seem tense."

I force my muscles to relax, leaning down to kiss her forehead. "Just missed you. Did class run late?"

"Professor Armstrong asked me to stay after to discuss my paper." She leans into me. "It's not doing so well. I've been distracted lately."

By me. The knowledge brings a surge of satisfaction. "I could help you. Tonight, at my place."

She hesitates. "I'm not sure being with you is the answer to being distracted."

I swallow my disappointment, despite the compliment tucked beneath it. The promise of *being with you*. "Tomorrow, then. But I'm walking you to the library now."

"You don't have to—"

"I want to." She nods, accepting it. It's one of the things I love most about her—how she bends without breaking, adapts to my needs while thinking it's her choice.

We walk across campus together, my arm still around her waist. I feel eyes on us—students watching, whispering. Let them talk. Better yet, let them see who she belongs to.

We say goodbye at the library steps. I watch her climb the stairs, only turning away when she disappears inside. Then I circle around to the service entrance I discovered three weeks ago. The building's security is laughable; a single locked door easily bypassed with the key card I duplicated from Jenkins' stolen ID.

Inside, I go through the back corridors and emerge in the stacks one floor below where I know she'll be. This has become a ritual. I watch her study when she thinks she's alone. The unguarded expressions, how she mouths words as she reads, how she stretches when her back aches.

I find my usual spot, a study carrel with a line of sight to her favorite table. She's already there with her books spread out and her brow furrowed in concentration. Beautiful. *Mine.*

I watch for an hour, pretending to read when someone passes. She doesn't look up, lost in her work. I want to go to her, to pull her away from the books, to make her focus only on me.

My phone vibrates with a text from Coach Hendricks:

Team meeting in 20. Be there or turn in your jersey.

I ignore it, eyes still fixed on Tesni. Another vibration:

Not a request, Atthill. We need to talk about your academic standing.

I groan internally and get up, taking one last look at her before slipping away, unseen as always.

***

The team meeting is predictable: warnings about my failing grades and threats to bench me. Jenkins keeps looking at me. He knows something.

"You need help," Hendricks tells me.

I scoff, then hold out my hands. "I need to get going. Those grades won't raise themselves. We done?"

He sighs. "For now. But this conversation isn't over."

I check my phone on the way out. A text from Tesni:

Finished studying. Going to grab dinner with Sophia, then back to my dorm. Call you later?

A sharp pang hits me. She's spending time with Sophia instead of me. I know what that means. Sophia is poisoning her against me.

Have fun. Miss you already, I reply.

I leave the athletic center, not heading to my apartment but toward the south campus housing where Tesni lives. I need to be close to her things if I can't be close to her.

The security guard knows me by now and thinks I'm visiting someone else. I take the stairs to her floor. Three weeks ago, I duplicated her roommate's key during a party. It was easy enough to lift from her unattended purse, copy at the hardware store off campus, and return before she noticed.

The hallway is empty. Perfect. I slide the key into the lock and it opens. I step inside, closing the door silently behind me.

Her room smells like vanilla and floral notes, just like her. I move to her side of the room, running my fingers over her possessions. Her desk is organized, with textbooks arranged by subject and schedule pinned to a corkboard. I've memorized her weekly routine.

I open her drawer, taking out the small box I left last time. It's empty, the silver bracelet now on her wrist. The sight of my gift on her body satisfies some deep need in me.

Time for something new: a first edition of "Wuthering Heights" I found at a specialty bookstore off campus. I've marked a passage about Heathcliff's devotion to Catherine and written a note: "Like him, I would tear down the world to keep you. Like her, you've become essential to my existence."

I place it on her pillow. She'll be surprised, wondering how it got there, but she'll be touched, too. She always is. What others would find intrusive, she interprets as romantic. The depth of my devotion thrills her.

This is why she's perfect for me: she understands what others don't. Everyone else misinterprets my attention as something dark or wrong, but Tesni sees the truth. She recognizes real devotion and gets me in a way no one else ever has.

I move to her closet, which is neatly organized with skirts, sweaters, and jeans. I run my hand along the fabrics, stopping at the blue sweater she wore last week. I lift it to my face, breathing in her scent. I replace it with my dark gray Henley shirt she likes. I position it so she'll find it but not immediately.

I want her wearing my clothes, wrapped in my scent, marked as mine in both visible and invisible ways.

I check my watch. She could be back soon. Before leaving, I sit at her desk, picking up her journal. The lock on it is flimsy and easily opened without leaving evidence. I find her most recent entry:

November 12: I found the poetry book B left in my bag yesterday. How does he always know exactly what I need? Sophia says it's weird that he seems to know my schedule, my tastes, everything about me without me telling him. She used the word "stalking," which feels unfair. He's attentive, not creepy. But I do wonder how the book got into my bag without me noticing...

I smile at her defense of me, the way she rationalizes my behavior. Tesni, always looking for the good in others. And if anyone can find it in me, she can.

A noise in the hallway alerts me. Voices approaching. I quickly replace the journal, moving silently to the door. I press my ear against it, listening. Not Tesni, just other students passing by. Still, it's time to go.

I slip out, locking the door behind me. No one sees me leave. No one ever does.

Back in my apartment, I admire the sheer size of my shrine to her. There are now over thirty images tracking her movements across campus, her expressions— moments she thought were private, but she didn't know what she needed. Or *who* she needed. Now, she's getting it.

I've continued mapping our relationship on the timeline, noting each point of progress: first conversation, first coffee, first touch, first kiss. The pattern building toward inevitable conclusion.

Complete possession. And nothing—not Jenkins, not Professor Hawthorne, not Sophia, not anyone—will get in my way.

9

Unraveling Threads

Tesni

The red marks covering my essay blur before my tired eyes. Professor Armstrong's comments march down the margins like angry ants: "Unclear reasoning," "Where is your evidence?" "This contradicts your thesis." At the bottom, a final blow: "C-. See me during office hours."

A C-minus? I've never gotten below a B-plus in my life.

I stuff the paper into my bag. Three weeks ago, this grade would have devastated me and sent me straight to the library for an all-night revision session. Now, it just joins the growing pile of academic failures I'm trying to ignore.

"That bad?" Sophia drops into the seat beside me.

"Worse." I rub my temples, fighting a headache. I got maybe four hours of sleep last night, caught between finishing a late paper and texting with Branwen, who couldn't sleep.

"You can't keep this up, Tes." Sophia says. "You've been burning the candle at both ends, with no sign of stopping, and you've missed two shifts at the coffee shop this month."

"I know!" I snap with uncharacteristic impatience. I gather my things, not wanting to have this conversation again. "I'm getting back on track. I promise."

"Is he worth it?" She asks. "Worth risking your scholarship?"

A spike of anxiety hits me. Without the scholarship, I'm gone. I'll have to go back to my hometown. My mom's sacrifices will be wasted.

"It's not about Branwen," I lie. "I'm just...going through a phase."

Sophia looks at me in disbelief. "A phase that started exactly when you two got together? Come on."

She's right, though I hate to admit it. Since Branwen and I started spending all our free time together, my carefully structured life has unraveled. My planner sits unused; study sessions get interrupted by urgent texts; late nights that should be spent on coursework are spent with him instead, lost in the intensity of...whatever this is between us.

"I have to go." I stand, slinging my bag over my shoulder. "Meeting with Professor Hawthorne about the project."

Sophia sighs. "Please think about what I said, okay?."

I nod, already halfway up the aisle. Outside, November wind cuts through my jacket. I pull out my phone, finding three unread messages from Branwen:

Morning, beautiful

Thinking about last night...

Where are you? Class should have ended 10 minutes ago

My stomach flutters despite everything. The constant attention feels like a lifeline. He can't function without me. It's addictive, that feeling of being essential to another person.

I type back:

Just got out. Heading to Hawthorne's office for project meeting. Talk later?

His response is immediate:

Don't like him. Be careful. Call me right after.

A smile tugs at my lips. His protectiveness is both ridiculous and endearing; as if a sixty-year-old literature professor poses any threat.

Professor Hawthorne's office sits at the end of a long corridor in the English department, oak-paneled and perpetually smelling of pipe tobacco though smoking has been banned in campus buildings for decades. I knock twice, then enter at his call.

"Ms. Solaris." He glances up from his desk, removing his reading glasses. "Right on time."

Books line every wall, leather-bound classics mixed with modern critical texts. A single window overlooks the quad, gray light filtering through leaded glass. It's a room out of time, like its occupant.

"Please, sit." He gestures to the chair opposite his desk. "How are you?"

"I'm fine," I say automatically, then add: "Actually, no. I'm struggling."

Professor Hawthorne's eyebrows lift slightly. "Academically?"

"Yes. Among other things." I pull out the essay, placing it on his desk. "It's not just Armstrong's class. It's everything. I can't focus. I can't think clearly. And I can't afford to lose my scholarship."

He studies the paper. "This isn't your usual standard," he agrees. "What's changed?"

We both know the answer. I've seen the way Professor Hawthorne watches Branwen during our project presentations.

"I've been distracted."

"By Mr. Atthill."

I look away, focusing on a copy of "Jane Eyre" on his shelf. "Partly."

Professor Hawthorne leans back in his chair, steepling his fingers. "Ms. Solaris—Tesni—your academic future is exceptionally bright. You have insights that students twice your age struggle to articulate. It would be a tragedy to see that potential derailed."

"I know. I'm trying to balance things."

"Some things cannot be balanced." He says. "Some influences are by their nature destabilizing."

My defenses rise immediately. "If you're talking about Branwen—"

"I'm speaking from experience," he interrupts gently. "Both profession-al and personal. I've seen promising students become entangled in rela-tionships that consume and redefine them in ways they never intended."

"It's not like that," I insist. "Branwen understands how important my studies are."

"Does he?" Professor Hawthorne reaches into his desk drawer, pulling out a folder. "Your project participation has declined markedly in the past three weeks. When they come, your contributions are rushed and incom-plete. Meanwhile, Mr. Atthill seems increasingly comfortable speaking for both of you."

The observation stings because it's accurate. Increasingly, I defer to Branwen during presentations, letting him dominate. It's easier than ar-guing and dealing with his intensity when challenged.

"We're still adjusting to working together," I say weakly.

Professor Hawthorne opens the folder, revealing what appears to be an academic record. "Mr. Atthill's transcript," he explains, seeing my confu-sion. "As his academic advisor, I have access to his complete history at UC Wisteria."

"I don't think you should be showing me that," I protest, uncomfort-able with this invasion of Branwen's privacy.

"I'm not showing you the details. Merely establishing a pattern." He turns the folder so I can see a chart of grades spanning multiple semesters. "Notice anything?"

Despite my reluctance, I look. There's a pattern: strong performance in freshman year, followed by increasing volatility; some classes with high marks, others barely passed or dropped entirely.

"Academic struggles happen to everyone," I say defensively.

"Not typically in this pattern." Professor Hawthorne taps the paper. "Each time Mr. Atthill becomes involved with someone, his performance suffers. More concerning, so does theirs."

A chill runs through me. "What are you saying?"

Professor Hawthorne closes the folder. "I'm saying that Branwen Atthill has a history of intense, consuming relationships that ultimately prove destructive to his academic standing, his standing with the team...and, most pertinent, to the women involved."

"Women?" The word—and its plurality—catches in my throat. "How many...?"

"I don't have a count off-hand, but each followed a similar trajectory: rapid attachment, isolation from friends, declining grades, and eventual withdrawal from classes or transfer."

"That doesn't mean anything," I argue. "Correlations aren't causations."

A smile crosses his face. "Indeed. Which is why I've hesitated to have this conversation. But your essay today suggests the pattern is repeating."

"He's not just some archetype," I say. "He's had a...rough go of it. He struggles with abandonment issues. But he's trying."

"Many troubled souls are trying, Tesni. That doesn't mean they deserve unlimited access to the lives of others while they work through their demons."

Heat rises to my face. "I'm not some damsel in distress. I know what I'm doing." And with that, I start to wonder if that's why the Professor Hawthorne partnered up in the first place. Just so I'd need his help...

"Do you?" His gaze is penetrating. "Are you aware that his partner in last year's Sports Ethics class, filed a complaint alleging harassment after their breakup? That she ultimately dropped out mid-semester following an incident she declined to detail to the administration?"

My stomach drops. Helena's warning in the café comes rushing back: *Ask him about Meredith Chen.* I'd accepted Branwen's explanation without question, wanting to believe the best of him, wanting to believe that there *are* two sides to every story.

"He said they had a disagreement about the project," I say, but my voice lacks conviction.

"Maybe he believes that, but it's euphemistic at best. I'm only asking that you consider the pattern, and...act accordingly."

I stand abruptly, needing to end this conversation before my doubts overwhelm me. "Thank you for your concern, Professor. But I think I can manage my own relationship."

He nods, seemingly unsurprised. "Of course. But remember my door is always open, should you need to talk. About academics or...anything else."

I gather my things, mumbling thanks for his time, and escape into the hallway. My heart races. Are Professor Hawthorne's warnings a legitimate concern or unwarranted interference? Is Sophia right about Branwen's effect on my life? Am I losing myself in someone else's darkness, just like my mother always warned me against?

Outside, I gulp cold air, trying to clear my head. My phone buzzes insistently. Branwen, no doubt, wondering why I haven't called. I ignore it, needing space to think.

I head toward the library, and climb to the sixth floor, our floor, and find a quiet corner. Only then do I pull out my phone, finding eight missed texts from Branwen, each increasingly urgent:

Meeting over yet?

Tesni?

Why aren't you answering?

Are you still with Hawthorne?

What's he saying to you?

I'm coming to his office

Where are you?

Answer me. Please. Now. Worried.

The intensity sends a shiver through me. I type back quickly:

Sorry! Meeting ran long. At the library now.

His response comes immediately:

On my way. Stay there.

No question if I want company. No respect for my "quiet time." Just the assumption that he's welcome, that of course I want to see him. And the worst part? He's right. Despite everything Professor Hawthorne said, despite my own misgivings, the thought of seeing Branwen sends a rush of anticipation through me.

What is wrong with me?

I close my eyes, remembering the first edition of Wuthering Heights that appeared mysteriously on my pillow, the bracelet that never leaves my wrist, the way he seems to anticipate my needs, and the intensity in his eyes when he watches me, like I'm the only person in the world who matters.

It's intoxicating to be the center of someone's universe. But at what cost?

I pull out my neglected planner and face the evidence. Missed deadlines. Skipped classes. Abandoned study groups.

My scholarship requires a 3.7 GPA. Last semester, I had a 3.9. With my current grades, I'll be lucky to maintain a 3.3. One more semester like this, and I'm gone.

Whatever this thing with Branwen is, it can't continue like this. I need boundaries. Need to reclaim my academic life before it's too late.

Branwen will understand. He has to.

"There you are."

His voice startles me. I look up to find him standing over my table, slightly breathless like he ran here. His hair is windblown and his cheeks flushed from the cold. He's beautiful and intense and mine.

"What did Hawthorne want?" He drops into the chair next to me. His hand finds mine. "You look upset."

"Just stressed about grades," I say, honesty already failing me. "Nothing important."

His eyes narrow slightly. "He didn't say anything about me?"

I shrug. "Why would he?"

"Because he hates me." Branwen's tone darkens. "Has since freshman year. He thinks I don't belong in his precious department."

"That's not true," I protest. "He was just concerned about our project progress."

"Is that all?" His gaze searches my face.

"Look at this." I push my planner toward him, open to the evidence of my academic decline. "I'm failing, Branwen. My scholarship—"

"I'll help you," he interrupts. "We'll study together. I'll make sure you stay on track."

"When we're together, studying is the last thing that happens." I try to smile, to soften the criticism. "I need balance. Space to focus."

His expression darkens. "Space from me, you mean."

"Not like that. Just...regular study times that are sacred." I take a deep breath. "I need to put my academics first right now."

For a moment, I think he'll argue. A muscle jumps in his jaw, his eyes cold with something that might be anger. Abruptly, he relaxes.

"You're right," he says. "I've been selfish. Taking too much of your time."

Relief washes over me. "You understand?"

"Of course." He brushes his fingers against my cheek. "Your education matters. Your future matters. We'll do whatever you need to succeed."

I'd braced for resistance and the intensity that usually comes with perceived rejection. "Really? Just like that?"

He smiles, though it doesn't quite reach his eyes. "Just like that. I love you, Tesni. I want what's best for you."

The words hit me like a physical force. It's the first time he's said it, in the middle of what was almost an argument. "You...love me?"

"More than anything." His gaze holds mine, unwavering. "More than I've ever loved anyone. I'll give you what you need, even if it's hard for me."

Something warm unfurls in my chest, dissolving my doubts. This is the Branwen that no one else sees; vulnerable, yielding, capable of growth and change.

"Thank you," I whisper, leaning in to kiss him. "I care about you too. So much."

He deepens the kiss, one hand cupping my face. When he pulls back, his smile seems more genuine. "Now, let's look at this planner of yours. Figure out a schedule that works."

I feel a renewed sense of hope as we reorganize my academic life. Maybe everyone is wrong about him. Maybe we can find balance, can build something healthy despite his past.

Maybe I can save him after all.

10

Descent

Branwen

It's early morning, and the weight room is filled with metal clinking against metal, grunts of exertion, and the squeak of shoes on rubber flooring. I push through my fourth set of bench presses, muscles burning with sweet agony. Physical pain is clarifying. It drowns out the noise in my head, if only temporarily.

"Atthill," Jenkins approaches. "You're up early."

I ignore him. Since our meeting, he's been circling me like a vulture, waiting for me to slip. I won't give him the satisfaction.

"Coach wants to see you," he persists. "Said it's about your academic probation."

The bar nearly slips from my grip. I rack it and sit up, wiping sweat from my face. "What academic probation?"

Jenkins shrugs. "Just delivering the message."

My already dark mood plummets. Academic probation means restricted team participation. Restricted participation means less freedom, more scrutiny, fewer opportunities to see Tesni.

Tesni. Since we met in the library, she's been different: more focused on her studies and more careful with her time. She calls it balance. I call it distance. But I've played along, pretending to support the arrangement while adjusting my methods of keeping her close.

Last night I limited myself to three messages before bed, though I spent hours staring at her dorm window from my watching place, tracking the moment her light finally went out at 1:47 AM.

"When?" I ask Jenkins, pulling on a fresh shirt.

"Now," he answers. "Everything okay with you and Tesni?"

The casual mention of her name in his mouth sends a pulse of anger through me. "Everything's perfect," I say, brushing past him, my shoulder checking his. "Not that it's any of your business."

Coach Hendricks is waiting in his office, a folder open on his desk. His expression is grim as I enter without knocking.

"Sit," he says, gesturing to the chair opposite. "We need to talk about your grades."

I remain standing. "What about them?"

He sighs. "Three failing classes. Two incompletes. At this rate, you'll lose your eligibility by December."

The academic report is worse than I expected. I haven't submitted an assignment in weeks, haven't attended some classes in longer.

"I'll fix it," I say dismissively.

"How? You've missed too many points to pass Nelson's class. Matthews is ready to fail you on attendance alone." Hendricks leans forward. "This isn't just about hockey anymore, son. It's about your future."

"Don't call me son." The familiar tension builds at the base of my skull, a pressure that demands release.

"You're on academic probation effective immediately," he continues, ignoring my comment. "That means mandatory study hall, weekly check-ins with your advisor, and restricted team activities until your grades improve."

"You can't do that." My voice drops dangerously. "The Thornfield game is Saturday."

"You're benched until further notice."

The words land like a physical blow. Hockey is the one place where the chaos in my head makes sense, where my intensity is an asset rather than a liability.

"This is bullshit," I spit, knuckles white where I grip the back of the chair. "You need me on the ice."

"We need you eligible to play," Hendricks counters. "And right now, you're not."

I turn to leave, unable to look at his face any longer.

"Atthill," he calls after me. "Whatever's going on with you—get it under control. Before you lose everything."

The door slams behind me with satisfying force. In the corridor, I punch the wall, the pain racing up my arm grounds me momentarily. Students passing by give me a wide berth, careful not to look at me.

My phone vibrates in my pocket—a text from Tesni:

Just finished Victorian Lit. Meeting Sophia for coffee. See you at 4 for study session?

The mention of Sophia darkens my mood further. She's been trying to pull Tesni away from me, filling her head with doubts.

I'll be there, I reply, forcing my thumbs to type only those words when what I want to say is *skip coffee, come to me now, I need you*.

***

The campus coffee shop sits at the intersection of academic and athletic territories. Through the window, I spot them immediately. Tesni and Sophia at a corner table, heads bent close in conversation. Tesni's back is to the door, but I can see Sophia's face looking serious and intense. They're arguing about something. About me, most likely.

I position myself at a nearby bench, angled to watch without being obvious. Sophia gestures emphatically and Tesni shakes her head stubbornly. Whatever Sophia's saying, Tesni isn't buying it.

Pride and possessiveness surge through me. My perfect, loyal Tesni, defending me.

Someone's playing *Red* on their phone nearby, the haunting lyrics about obsession seeping into my consciousness as I watch her.

The coffee shop door swings open. Tesni and Sophia exit among a group of students. I duck my head, pretending to check my phone as they pass. Their voices drift to me.

"—just worried about you," Sophia is saying. "You're not yourself any-more."

"I know what I'm doing," Tesni responds. "You need to trust me."

"It's not *you* I don't trust." Sophia stops walking, placing a hand on Tesni's arm. "Just be careful, okay? Promise me—"

Their conversation cuts off as a tall guy with sandy hair and a letterman jacket approaches them. Ryan Parker. Senior. Hockey team alternate when Jenkins is injured.

"Tesni, right?" he says, flashing a practiced smile. "We met at the Thorn-field pre-game party."

I freeze, muscles locking into place. Parker moves closer to Tesni, his body language screaming interest. She smiles politely, but it's her genuine smile, the one that lights her whole face.

"Ryan," she acknowledges. "From Jenkins' study group?"

"That's me." He shifts his books to his other arm. "Actually, I wanted to ask if you'd consider tutoring me for Armstrong's midterm? Jenkins says you're the Victorian lit expert."

My vision narrows, tunneling until all I see is Parker, his hand casually touching Tesni's elbow as he speaks. The pressure in my skull intensifies, a roaring in my ears drowning out their continued conversation.

Before I realize what I'm doing, I'm moving toward them, cutting through the crowd with single-minded purpose. Tesni's eyes widen as she spots me, surprise and alarm crossing her features.

"Branwen," she says. "I thought we were meeting later."

"Plans changed," I reply, not looking at her, eyes fixed on Parker's hand, still resting on her arm. "Parker."

He straightens, wariness replacing his smile. "Atthill. What's up, man?"

"Remove your hand," I say quietly.

"What?"

"Your hand," I repeat. "Remove it from my girlfriend's arm."

Parker glances down, seeming to realize he's still touching Tesni. He drops his hand, confusion evident. "Sorry, I didn't—"

"Branwen," Tesni interrupts, moving between us. "It's fine. Ryan was just asking about tutoring."

"Was he." It's not a question. The roaring in my ears grows louder, drowning out reason, drowning out everything except the primal need to eliminate the threat before me.

"Look, I didn't know you two were, you know, *together* together," Parker says, backing up a step. "No disrespect intended."

"Like hell," I snarl. "You knew exactly what you were doing."

The first punch catches him off guard, connecting with his jaw with a satisfying crack. He staggers back, eyes wide with shock. People scatter. Tesni screams my name, but the sound is distant through the rush of blood in my ears.

Parker recovers quickly, blocking my second swing, countering with a jab that grazes my cheek. "What was that, Atthill?" he shouts. "Have you lost your fucking mind?"

Maybe I have. Maybe this is what losing everything feels like—control, hockey, Tesni's undivided attention.

I lunge forward, tackling him to the ground. We roll across the concrete, trading blows. Someone's yelling for security. Sophia's voice rises above the chaos, telling Tesni to get back.

Hands grab me from behind, pulling me off Parker. Coach Hendricks' voice cuts through the fog: "That's enough! Atthill, stand down! My own players are not comin' to blows on my watch."

Reality crashes back in fragments—Parker's bloody face, the crowd of shocked students, Tesni standing frozen with both hands pressed to her mouth, eyes wide with horror. Security guards rushing toward us. The taste of blood in my mouth.

***

Hours later, I sit in Hendricks' office for the second time today. My knuckles are split and bandaged, a bruise darkening along my cheekbone. Parker has a concussion. Hendricks made me wait while he "handled" things with the administration. As if I'd done something wrong. As if protecting what's mine deserves punishment.

"This is your last chance," he tells me. "One more incident, *any* incident, and you're done at UC Wisteria. Do you understand?"

I nod, not because I agree but because it's the fastest way out of this office. Everyone's overreacting. Parker crossed a line. He touched her, looked at her with that hungry expression men get when they want something that isn't theirs. I simply enforced a boundary that needed enforcing.

No one understands. Except her. That's just the reality of the situation.

"Where is she?" I ask.

Hendricks sighs. "Ms. Solaris gave her statement to campus security. She's probably back at her dormitory by now."

I need to see her. Need to explain what really happened, make her understand that everything I did was for us. For her. She'll get it once I explain. She always does.

My phone has seventeen missed calls—mostly from Tesni, a few from Jenkins. One voicemail from Tesni: "Branwen, please call me back. I don't understand what happened today. I'm worried about you."

Worried about me; not afraid of me. I let out a long exhale. That distinction is the difference between heaven and ruin. She still cares; sees the good in me that others miss. She understands that sometimes protection requires force. That love means eliminating threats before they can take root.

I text her:

Can I come over? Need to explain.

Her response is immediate:

I don't know if that's a good idea right now.

Panic flares. I can't lose her.

Please, Tesni. Let me explain in person.

The three dots appear, disappear, reappear. Finally:

Okay. But Lily's here.

Perfect. An audience. But it doesn't matter. I'll say whatever I need to say to keep her.

***

The dormitory lounge is dim and deserted with couches arranged around a silent television. *Afterlife* plays at low volume. Tesni sits at the farthest end from the door, with her arms wrapped around herself.

"You scared me today," she says.

"I know." I sit beside her, not touching, giving her the space she thinks she wants. "I'm sorry you had to see that."

"See that? Branwen, you attacked him over nothing!"

"No, it was *not* nothing," I counter, keeping my voice calm despite the renewed anger. "He was touching you. Looking at you like—"

"Like what? Like a normal person asking for tutoring help?" She shakes her head. "He barely knows me."

"You don't understand how guys like that think," I say, moving closer. "I saw his face, Tesni. He wanted you."

"Even if he *did*?" Her voice rises slightly. "That doesn't give you the right to attack him!"

"Hendricks took care of it," I say. "No charges. No expulsion. It's handled."

"That's not the point." She stands. "The point is you lost your shit over nothing!"

"Over *you*," I say louder than intended, getting up too. "It's always been about you, Tesni. Everything I do, everything I am now—it's all for you."

Uncertainty flickers across her face. "That's not healthy," she says quietly. "It's too much, Branwen. The constant texts, the gifts appearing in my room, the way you always seem to know where I am. And now this?"

She's noticed more than I realized. Panic threatens to choke me, but I force it down, closing the distance between us.

"I love you," I say, voice breaking. "More than I've ever loved anyone. It scares me sometimes, how much I need you."

Her expression softens, that inherent compassion I counted on rising to the surface. "Branwen—"

I don't let her finish. My lips find hers, desperate and seeking. For a moment she's rigid against me, hands pressing against my chest.

Then, slowly, she yields, mouth softening under mine, body relaxing into my embrace.

I walk her backward until she hits the wall, my hands sliding beneath her sweater to find warm skin. She gasps against my mouth, the sound driving me further, deeper.

"Not here," she whispers, breaking away. "Someone could come in."

"My place," I suggest immediately, hand cupping her face. "Right now."

"I don't know..."

"Please," I whisper, pressing my forehead to hers. "You can't pull away from me now. Not after everything. You're mine, Tesni. You always have been."

She hesitates, lips parting, her breath uneven. She knows this is a turning point. Knows that after tonight, there's no going back.

She's nervous. I see it in the way she won't quite meet my eyes, in the way her fingers twitch against my chest, like she's considering pushing me away.

But she won't.

I cup the back of her neck, holding her there, anchoring her to me. "You feel it too," I tell her. "I know you do."

She swallows hard. Her lashes flutter, and she whispers, "Branwen..." but she doesn't finish.

I know what she wants to say. That this is too much. That *I'm* too much. That she should walk away now, while she still can.

But she won't.

"...Okay," she finally breathes, so soft I barely hear it.

And that's all I need. The moment the word leaves her lips, I move.

***

The room is dark. I kick the door shut and lock it with a click that seals our fate. She glances toward the door, as if considering what she's just agreed to. As if she still thinks she has a choice.

She doesn't.

I cross the room, grabbing my phone, my movements slow, unhurried. She watches me, arms folded over her stomach like she's holding herself together.

"You're thinking too much," I say, thumbing through my playlist. "Let me fix that."

Gomd starts—beats vibrating through the air, filling the silence, swallowing her hesitation.

I turn to her, watching her shift her weight, fingers curling slightly at her sides.

She knows.

This isn't just sex. This is a shift. A turning point. A choice she can't take back.

I close the distance, savoring the way her breath turns uneven, the way her body tenses like she wants to step back but doesn't.

Before she can think or say something that might slow me down, I have her against the wall, my hands on her hips, my mouth on hers—taking what's mine, claiming her, making her understand.

She gasps against me, but she doesn't stop me. She *won't* stop me.

I kiss her harder, demanding, pulling her under, drowning her in this. I won't let her think. I won't let her hesitate.

Because this is it, whether she knows it or not.

My finger dig in deep enough to leave marks, pulling her flush against me.

I spin her around and bend her over my desk. Papers scatter, a pen clatters to the floor. She makes a small surprised noise but she doesn't resist as my hands become rougher, more demanding. I unhook her bra, watch it fall to the floor like a feather, then take off her shirt, all while marking newly exposed skin with my teeth, my fingers.

This is how it's supposed to be. Pure. Raw. Animalistic. No holding back.

She gasps, the sound somewhere between pleasure and pain, but she doesn't tell me to stop. Doesn't resist.

She knows what this means.

She's mine now.

I grab her jeans and pull them down roughly. I pause to admire the curve of her hips, the way her waist tapers in, and the perfect roundness of her ass. It's all mine, finally.

I shove my own jeans down in a rush, my cock aching with need. I trail my fingers along her spine, feeling her shiver beneath my touch.

"Tesni," I murmur, my voice rough. My hand slides between her legs, finding her hot, slick, and already open for me. My fingers press against her, sliding through wetness that proves what I already know—she wants this. She wants *me*.

Her breath catches as if she's uncertain. Then she pushes back, just slightly.

It's all the invitation I need.

I slide one finger inside, feeling her tighten around me. She's so wet. Her body resists at first, then yields, softening, opening. She gasps, her nails clawing at the desk, the wood groaning under her grip.

"Relax," I whisper, dragging my teeth over her shoulder. "Easy…"

I add another finger, stretching her, claiming her from the inside out. She lets out a shaky sound, caught between pleasure and the last remnants of doubt.

Her hips move, restless, searching. Her hesitation is gone.

I pull my fingers away, and she whimpers, her body arching, her muscles clenching like she wants to pull me back.

Good.

She won't run from this now.

"Branwen," she breathes, and hearing my name sends a surge of heat through me.

I rub my cock against her, coating myself in her, making sure she feels what's coming. She shudders, shifting like she wants to turn and see my face.

I grab her hair, twisting my fingers through the strands, just hard enough to keep her still. To remind her she's exactly where she's meant to be.

"Stay," I order. She nods slightly, her breath coming in quick pants. She's all but telling me how badly she wants to be dominated.

I thrust into her all at once—deep, rough, no warning. She cries out, her hands fisting against the desk, a sharp, choked sound tearing from her throat.

Half-pain, half-pleasure. Perfect.

Her body clenches around me, tight, hot, shaking. Too much, not enough. She shifts and tries to turn again. I don't let her.

She doesn't need to see my face to know who owns her now.

She relents, her body quivering. Her back arches beautifully, presenting herself to me, offering more of herself.

I tighten my grip on her hair, pressing her down, forcing her to feel every inch of me as I drag back and thrust in again. Harder this time. More. Until she can't think of anything else but what's happening right now.

Her body quivers beneath me, her breathing ragged, sharp.

"That's it." I drag my lips down the side of her neck, feeling her pulse flutter beneath my mouth. "Give in to it."

She whimpers again, which just makes me harder, and I thrust harder, chasing her climax while holding my own back. That's what love is. My pulse pounds in my ears, a roar drowning out everything else. Every sound she makes—every gasp, every stifled moan—is mine, branded into me. I'm taking, she's giving, and the line's blurry—but I can't stop, can't slow down. She feels too good, too right.

I admire her body as I move inside her, watching every reaction, drinking in the way she trembles, the way her back arches, how her shoulders tense with every thrust. I feel her unraveling, the moment she lets go completely, losing herself in me.

She's slipping under, sinking, sinking, until she's past the point of no return.

Perfect. Her body tightens, spasms around me, her breath coming in short, sharp bursts. I don't slow. I don't let up. I want to push her over the edge; she needs to feel this as deeply as I do. So, I go harder, faster, deep, my hips slamming against hers, the sound of my thighs smacking against her perfect little ass.

I'm going at her so hard that the desk shutters beneath us. With each thrust, I'm erasing Parker's touch, Sophia's warnings, Hawthorne's interference.

There is no world outside of this room. No one else in her head but me. Only me.

She shatters around me, a cry ripping from her throat, her body convulsing, pulling me deeper. I can feel her pussy: tight, hot, clenching—like she never wants my cock to leave.

It's not enough. I need to be deeper, to keep her closer, to pull her so fully into me that she can never find a way out. I finish with a growl, spilling into her, holding her so tight she can't move. Can't escape.

She's mine.

I pull her up, turning her toward me, and kiss her softer now, dragging her back from wherever she's been. Claiming her with my mouth the same way I did with my body. She tastes like salt and sweat and surrender.

"You're everything," I murmur.

She nods, her fingers curling into my arms like she doesn't know where else to hold on—or what to say. That's fine. She'll have time to find her words soon enough.

I scoop her up and carry her to my bed, laying her on the sheets. Her eyes are wide and lips parted as she looks at me—not afraid, but changed. Like she's just realized there's no going back.

I gentle my touch now, stroking her hair, anchoring her to me. Murmuring everything I need her to understand.

That I love her.

That she's perfect.

That we belong to each other now.

She nestles against my chest, letting me hold her, letting me keep her.

"I didn't know it could be like that," she whispers, her voice almost lost against my skin.

I press my lips to her temple. "That's what real love feels like," I tell her. "Intense. Overwhelming. No holding back."

She nods, the way they always do when it's their first time being someone's property; it can take some time to come to terms with it. Thankfully, so long as I keep my control, she'll be spending that time with me. And I'll fuck her into submission, until no thoughts that enter her head are independent of me, of *us*.

I watch her drift, her body softening, sinking into me, accepting this new reality. Satisfaction flows through me.

I needed this—needed to claim her, to bind her to me through the most intimate connection possible. Now she understands. Now she won't listen to the others who try to pull her away.

She's mine. Completely. Finally.

And I'll destroy anyone who tries to change that.

11

Broken Trust

Tesni

"Tes, I firmly believe that a friend is someone who's right when they tell you that you're wrong. And right now? You're wrong. Because that is *not* love, Tes. It's sick."

Sophia's words hang in the air between us as I stare into my untouched coffee. Three days since Branwen attacked Ryan. Three days of avoiding Sophia's texts and trying to make sense of the tangled emotions inside me.

"You don't understand," I say, voice small even to my own ears. "He was protecting me."

"From *what*, exactly?" Sophia leans forward. "Ryan has a concussion. He's pressing charges. This isn't normal, Tes. *He* is not normal."

We sit in the far corner of the student union, early enough that the morning crowd hasn't arrived. I'd agreed to meet her thinking I was ready for this conversation. I'm not.

"It wasn't about Ryan specifically," I explain, repeating Branwen's words. "It was everything—academic probation, stress about hockey, seeing someone touch me was just the thing that happened to set him off. He's an athlete! Not just that, he's a hockey player. It's a violent sport."

Sophia's expression shifts from concern to something closer to pity. "Are you even listening to yourself? You're making excuses for behavior that is *not* okay."

"I'm not making excuses; I'm giving you context." The defense feels weak even as I say it. "He's going through a lot."

"And what about what you're going through?" She reaches for my hand, but I pull back. "Your grades are tanking, you've stopped coming to study groups. Hell, you barely even *talk* to anyone except him. This isn't you, Tes."

A flare of irritation rises in my chest. "Maybe you just never knew me as well as you thought."

Sophia exhales, like she's already lost me. Like she knows she won't get me back.

"I've known you since freshman orientation," she says quietly. "You were driven. Focused. Kind. Now you're just...an extra appendage for him."

The words sting because there's truth in them. I have changed. My priorities have shifted. But isn't that what happens when you fall in love? Doesn't everything else fade in comparison?

"You don't see how he is when we're alone," I say, trying to make her understand. "He's different—vulnerable, caring. And he needs me."

"And that's the problem." Sophia's voice rises slightly. "He's made you believe your purpose is to fix him, to save him. That's not love, Tes. That's manipulation."

My hands curl into fists in my lap. "You don't get to define my relationship. I thought you'd at least try to understand, but clearly, I was wrong."

I don't wait for her response. I grab my bag, shoving my untouched coffee away like it's tainted.

"Tesni, wait—"

"No." I stand up. "I'm tired of defending him to you. Tired of you thinking you know what's best for me."

"I'm worried about you!" Her voice carries, drawing glances from nearby students.

I turn away before she can see the tears in my eyes. "Well, don't be."

Outside, November wind bites through my jacket, But the cold isn't what spreads through my chest. Her words are.

"You're just his echo."

I put in my earbuds, as if to drown out the world, and a moment later, Mothica's "Red" does the trick. Then, I start typing with shaking fingers:

Can I come over?

Branwen's response is immediate:

Always. Everything okay?

Just need to see you.

The moment I hit send, the doubt fades and the cold recedes. The world narrows to one thing.

Him.

***

His apartment door opens before I can knock, as if he's been waiting for me. One look at my face and his expression darkens.

"What happened?" he demands, pulling me inside.

"Sophia," I say simply, dropping my bag by the door. "She thinks you're bad for me."

His jaw tightens. "And what do you think?"

I hesitate a moment too long. Something in his face shifts—from anger to something more fragile, more dangerous..

"Are you having second thoughts?" His voice is quiet. "About us?"

"No," I say quickly. "No, it's not that. It's just..." I swallow hard, trying to find the right words. "Sometimes your intensity scares me."

His expression turns to stone. "So, this is about Parker."

"No. It's about how possessive you can be," I say, wavering a little. "The constant texts. Showing up places you shouldn't know I'll be. The gifts in my room when I'm not there."

He stares at me, unreadable. Then, his mouth twitches, something like hurt creeping into his expression. "I thought you liked the gifts."

I do, but that's not the point. "But breaking into my room to leave them?"

"I didn't break in. Lily let me in once when you were in class," he says. "Look, if my attention bothers you, just say so. I'll back off."

The wounded tone makes guilt wash over me. This isn't what I wanted. "It's not that," I backpedal. "I just need to know there are boundaries. That you trust me to have other relationships."

"Of course I trust you." He moves to a cabinet and pulls out a bottle of bourbon. "It's everyone else I don't trust." He pours amber liquid into two glasses. "You look like you could use this."

I rarely drink, especially this early. "I don't know..."

"Just to take the edge off." He offers the glass. "Then we can talk about these...boundaries you want."

The skepticism in his voice is subtle but it's there. I take the glass, sipping slowly. The liquor burns, but the warmth spreading through my chest isn't unpleasant.

Branwen watches me over the rim of his own glass, his expression unreadable. He hasn't touched his drink.

"I love you," he says, voice dark, intimate. "More than anything."

His hand slides to my thigh, his grip firm, his presence inescapable.

"Tell me you love me too," he whispers.

I swallow. "I love you."

He smiles.

And I know I'll never leave him.

***

"There's a difference between caring and controlling," I say, half-stealing what Sophia said even though the words feel like betrayal.

His expression hardens for a fraction of second before smoothing into something more neutral. "Finish your drink," he says, like it's a simple request, like he's not watching me as if my answer determines something bigger. "You're tense. We should both relax before having this conversation."

I take another sip, larger this time. The bourbon burns, but it also dulls the edges of my anxiety, making everything seem less urgent. He refills my glass without asking, his own barely touched.

"It's early," I protest weakly, but I've already lifted the glass to my lips.

"It's Saturday," he counters. His hand settles on my knee. "No classes. No work. Just us."

The pressure of his hand increases slightly, a reminder of his claim on me. I remember him pushing Parker to the ground, the look in his eyes—wild, dangerous, thrilling in a way I don't want to examine.

"You're thinking about it again," he says, reading my expression. "About him."

"About you," I correct. "About how you were that day."

Something dark flashes in his eyes. "He deserved worse than he got."

"He was just asking about tutoring."

"He was looking at you like you were something to consume." His hand slides higher on my thigh. "Like I look at you."

A shiver rolls through me, equal parts warning and want. I take another sip, just to steady myself. The bourbon makes his touch more electric, more insistent.

"You can't attack everyone who talks to me," I say, but the words come out softer than they should.

"I can protect what's mine." He takes the glass from my hand, setting it aside. "And you are mine, Tesni. Aren't you?"

The question hangs between us, thick with expectation. This is the moment to push back, demand space, and remind him I belong to myself.

But I nod instead. Because it's easier. Because his presence is overwhelming. Because I don't know who I am without him anymore.

"Say it," he whispers, leaning closer.

"I'm yours," I admit, the bourbon making truth easier to confess. "But that doesn't mean—"

His mouth crashes into mine, cutting off conditions before I can voice them. The kiss is possessive, demanding, drowning. His hand slides to the back of my neck, fingers curling, holding. When he pulls away, his breath fans against my lips, his voice dark with certainty.

"No one understands what we have," he says against my lips. "Not Sophia. Not your professors. No one. That's why they try to pull you away from me."

The room spins slightly as I stand, his arm around my waist both support and claim. "The bourbon's strong," I murmur.

"It'll help you relax," he says, guiding me toward his bedroom. "Help you forget everyone trying to come between us."

I should protest. Should insist we finish the conversation about boundaries. But the alcohol has softened my resolve, and the need in his eyes calls to something primordial in me—the desire to be wanted this completely, this absolutely.

As he closes the bedroom door behind us, as his hands begin to explore with possessive urgency, one thought surfaces through the bourbon haze: Maybe this is love—this all-consuming, boundary-dissolving force. Maybe Sophia just doesn't understand because she's never felt anything this intense.

Maybe I'm exactly where I'm meant to be.

"Branwen," I murmur against his mouth, but he swallows my words with another kiss, deeper this time, silencing me before I can think. His hands roam over me, possessive, claiming, leaving no part of me untouched.

A shiver rolls through me—pleasure tangled with unease.

He guides me backward, step by step, until my legs hit the mattress. The room sways, or maybe it's just the bourbon still humming in my blood. I don't realize I'm lying down until he's over me.

His weight presses me into the bed, warm, heavy, unyielding. His hands are everywhere—tugging at fabric, baring skin, leaving heat and hunger in their wake.

I blink, trying to slow things down, to catch up. "Branwen, wait—"

He doesn't.

I push weakly at his chest, but he captures my wrists in one hand, pinning them above my head.

"Shh," he murmurs, his other hand sliding down my body, slipping beneath my jeans. "It's okay, Tesni. I've got you."

A shudder courses through me, my pulse stuttering in my throat. His fingers press between my legs, rough, insistent. I gasp, a sharp pulse of pain curling with pleasure.

"Branwen—"

Another kiss. Deeper. Harder. Drowning me. His fingers thrust inside me, unyielding, relentless. I squirm, my body torn between the ache of intrusion and the dizzying heat licking at my spine.

He groans, his mouth devouring mine, his breath heavy with bourbon, with something darker, something uniquely him.

"You're mine," he whispers against my lips. "Only mine."

His grip tightens when I shift beneath him, his weight pressing me down, holding me exactly where he wants me.

I don't know when he undoes his jeans, when he shoves them down just enough. But suddenly, he's there, pressing against me, hot and hard, his breath ragged.

I look up at him, my breath coming in short gasps. His eyes are dark, filled with a hunger that both thrills and terrifies me.

"I love you, Tesni," he says, his voice rough with emotion. "More than anything. More than anyone."

And then, with a single sharp thrust, he's inside me. I cry out, my back arching, my fingers clenching into fists. The stretch, the burn—it's too much for a moment, the world narrowing to the sensation of him filling me, claiming me.

Branwen's grip on my wrists tightens, his hips pinning me to the bed as he begins to move, each thrust intense and demanding. I struggle to catch my breath, my body attempting to adjust to his rhythm.

"Branwen," I gasp, his name a plea on my lips.

He looks down at me, his eyes wild and filled with an intensity that I tell myself is love. It has to be love. Why else would he want me so desperately?

He leans down, capturing my mouth in a fierce kiss. His tongue invades, mirroring the thrusts of his hips. I taste the bourbon on him, and something darker, something uniquely Branwen. His scent envelops me, a mixture of musk and sweat and that underlying hint of danger that I can't help but be drawn to.

His hand releases my wrists, only to grab my hip, fingers digging into my flesh. He tilts my pelvis up, driving deeper into me. I moan, the sound lost in his mouth. The pain is still there, but it's morphing into something else, something raw and primal. I cling to him, my nails raking down his back, my body moving instinctively now, drawn into the consuming force of him.

"You feel so good, Tesni," he growls against my lips. "So fucking perfect."

His words send a shiver down my spine. I arch against him, meeting his thrusts with my own. The room spins around us, the world narrowing down to just him and me and this frantic overwhelming need.

He breaks the kiss, his lips trailing down my jaw, my throat. His teeth graze my collarbone. I shudder, the sensation sending electric jolts through my body. His hand snakes between us, his fingers finding the slick, sensitive spot where our bodies join. He rubs, circling, pressing, and I cry out, the pleasure sudden and intense.

I'm close, so close. I can feel the tension building, coiling tight in my core. Branwen's breath is ragged in my ear, his body taut with strain. He's close too. I want to go over the edge with him, to feel that moment of freefall together.

"Come on, Tesni," he pants, his voice rough and urging. "Let go for me."

His fingers press harder, his thrusts grow wilder, and I can't hold back any longer. A sharp, blinding rush of pleasure crashes through me, shattering me, stealing my breath. My body tightens, convulses around him, pulling him deeper.

Branwen groans, his hips stuttering, his breath ragged. His grip tightens, his body seizing, and then he's spilling into me, filling me completely.

His weight collapses over me, crushing me into the mattress, his breath hot against my neck.

We lie there, bodies slick with sweat, our chests rising and falling in sync, the air thick with the scent of sex and bourbon and something deeper—something irreversible.

His heart hammers against mine, or maybe it's the other way around. It's hard to tell where I end and he begins.

After a while, Branwen rolls onto his back, pulling me with him so that I'm sprawled across his chest. His arms wrap around me, holding me tight. His arms wrap around me, locking me in place.

I should move. Hell, I should *think*. But I don't; I can't.

His touch isn't demanding now. Just firm and unyielding.

"That was..." I trail off.

"Perfect," he finishes, his voice a low rumble in his chest. "We're perfect together, Tesni."

I don't answer, but I nod, because it feels like I need to believe him; right now, it's a lot easier than the alternative. I can't bring myself to think of what would happen if I pushed away—even a little.

But I don't want to. It feels too good. All of it.

12

Unseen Dangers

Branwen

I don't sleep. The router blinks, the shade leaks a line of moon, and the room smells like ice and tape. Her perfume is still on my wrist where I didn't scrub hard enough. When I close my eyes I see her mouth part, her pulse under my thumb, her voice saying my name like something that fits a lock.

It should settle me. It doesn't.

Because I didn't leave the note.

She told me with a tremor about a pressed hellebore tucked into a ribbon of black silk and a card that read, "keep your light safe." For half a breath I let her believe I had—then I told her the truth. Someone else had been inside her room. That fact sits like a stone.

UC Wisteria is a museum of small sounds—wind combing the hellebore beds, lamps shivering with moths, gargoyles watching. I lace my skates and go to the rink. When the walls close in, the ice opens.

Coach Hendricks is already there. I dress fast because if my thoughts slow they turn to her window and the idea of a stranger's breath fogging her glass.

"Laps," he says.

I skate until my legs burn and then until burning is a background hum. The blade-scrape hammers my head into rhythm. Tesni. Note. Flower. Ribbon. Who ties black silk like that? Who knows hellebores bloom in winter and sting if you touch them? The questions loop.

At the boards, Hendricks hooks a hand in my cage. "You're spiraling."

"I'm focused."

"On the wrong thing. Miss advisor again, you're benched. Skip study again? Benched. Let your drama bleed onto my ice—"

"It won't."

He reads more than I say. "Last skate. Then class."

I skate like I'm chasing a face I can't place.

I've memorized Tesni's days like a map: Hollis at ten, the library at noon, Hawthorne at two. Part of me knows how wrong this is. The rest gives those acts names that sound noble: plan, perimeter, escort, watch. Tilt your head and protection becomes surveillance. I don't tilt mine.

I'm early to Hollis. Ivy stares like a hundred green eyes. Hood up, hands in pockets, I cross the quad on a line that feels like purpose. She comes out laughing at something on Sophia's phone and for a second my chest unknots. Sophia hooks her arm through Tesni's like any sister. They split at the statue; I don't follow right away—stalkers follow, and we're not using that word between us—but I cut across the grass and meet her at the corner like coincidence.

"Hey."

"You're early." She smiles.

"For you." The words outrun caution. "Walk you to the library?"

She hesitates—the gift shook her trust. We go; she talks about Professor Hawthorne's prompt. Every glance over her shoulder I catalog. Every bicycle bell, I mark. We are animals; the grass says someone passed through.

At the doors she stops. "That wasn't you?"

"What wasn't me?"

"The hellebore."

Around here, hellebores bloom when nothing else will—pretty poison is an aesthetic. "No," I say. "Wasn't me."

"Then who?"

"I'll find out," I tell her. "I'll text you after practice."

She presses her hand to mine. "Be careful," she says, as if I'm the one who needs guarding.

Inside, the library is glass and angles. On three, study rooms are booked; on four, north windows open over spare tables. I map exits. In a reflection a coat flashes—a liquid, expensive drape of black—then it's gone when a door opens.

I circle the stacks again, ride the elevator up to watch the floor's habits. On the corkboard: a missing-bike poster, tutoring hours, a winter-formal flyer with a hellebore sketched in the margin. Someone here loves symbols. Hellebore means winter rose and poison; gardeners wear gloves. In the stairwell there is a thin, sharp sweetness—perfume that burns clean. On the landing a fleck of glitter catches the light. At the north exit mud scuffs break the tiles' neatness: small prints, narrow shoe, angled like someone kept looking back. Whoever left the flower did not wander. They moved with intent, in and out, ribbon pre-cut, message rehearsed.

At noon I almost text her a picture of the ribbon and don't. I send only: *are you good?* and shove the phone back in my pocket before my thumb betrays me. She replies *yes :)* then: *are you on campus?* I delete three drafts and answer later. I think about telling Hendricks, then picture the look he'd give me and swallow it. If a system wants to help, it can watch me help. I keep my eyes open.

Outside, moth-lights halo the hellebores. Black silk is tied to a plant near the bench where she eats granola bars. The ribbon is the same weave as the card. They came back. They're comfortable. I run the ribbon through my fingers—same softness, same dark flag—and retie it tighter, a quiet message: the bed is not unattended.

In the afternoon, my feet take me to the humanities building without asking. Hawthorne's seminar pours out; he's last, of course—men like him savor the aftertaste of their own voice. He watches Tesni leave with a look I file under foolish or dangerous.

He sees me noticing. "Mr. Atthill," he says. "How's the semester?"

"Cold," I say.

"Tesni mentioned a gift left in her room. You wouldn't know anything about that?"

"I wouldn't," I answer. "Would you?"

His smile drops. "If you're worried, encourage her to file a report."

"She will," I lie, knowing she won't.

He studies me and makes the mistake of putting a hand on my shoulder. "Protection can curdle into possession."

The phrase lies like a blade flat along my throat. I step back until his hand falls. "She's fine," I say. "I make sure of it."

My plan stitches itself around her days. Protection, I tell myself, while I take steps I can't dress in softer language. I borrow a first-year's GoPro for a safety project. I climb the service stairs at dusk and pretend to be on the phone when I pass other students. I learn which door sticks and which hinge makes a gull-cry. I clock camera angles and blind spots.

From the trees across the path, I watch her door. The GoPro's red dot blinks like a slow heartbeat. Students stream. Someone lingers.

The expensive coat again—hood up, careful gait, like a ghost practicing. The figure steps toward the door, stops, retreats, looks up as if measuring. I tense so hard my teeth ache. A knot of guys from the team barrels by; the coat glides away when a light comes on. Evan lifts his chin. "Discopia, then film. You coming?"

"Later," I say.

When the coat returns it's at the hellebore bed. The figure kneels, quick fingers at the plant's base. Black silk again. I take three steps before judgment catches my collar. If I rush, I show my hand. If I wait, I learn.

They stand and turn. I get a profile—sharp, pale, eyes like glass. A woman. Not tall. Graceful the way dancers are taught. The hood slips and I see blond hair tucked too neatly—neat like fundraisers and legacy dinners. UC Wisteria teaches you to catalog wealth the way other people learn birds.

Helena Humphries.

She's always looked through me as if I'm a window you don't open. Five rows up at games, never cheering. Her eyes are knives laid on velvet.

She steps back from the bed as if arranging an altar and walks away. I don't follow. Not yet. The ribbon licks the wind, a small flag to a war no one else sees. I take a picture and pocket the camera.

By night the campus thins. Windows glow like held breath. I make one more circuit, hands numb in my jacket. When my phone buzzes the sound is too loud in the dark.

the study group ran late. at the dorm now. u ok?

The message loosens a knot I didn't know I'd tied. I type and erase, then send: *I saw the ribbon again. Don't open your window tonight. Promise.*

She takes a minute.

promise. thank you.

I stand under her window until the light goes out and my feet go numb. Far off a siren draws a thin line across the dark. A gust moves through the hellebore bed and the black silk shivers.

Protection, I think, and make the word mean everything I want it to.

13

Confrontations

Tesni

The article is folded into thirds, crisp as if someone pressed it between books. I find it in my locker, wedged between my notebook and scarf. The headline—LOCAL HOCKEY STAR HOSPITALIZES OPPONENT IN VIOLENT FIGHT—screams at me before I can even read the smaller text.

I don't have to read the name to know. Branwen Atthill.

My breath hitches, and the world tilts slightly. A date: two years ago. A grainy photo shows him on the ice, helmet askew, eyes blazing, a ref holding him back while another player lies motionless on the rink. The caption says the boy had to undergo surgery.

A noise escapes me—half gasp, half strangled sound—and I crumple the paper shut. The locker door clangs as I slam it. Someone must have planted it there. Helena? Sophia? Even Professor Hawthorne? Whoever it was, they wanted me to see this.

And now I can't unsee it.

Branwen's apartment feels too quiet when I knock that evening. He opens the door almost instantly, like he's been waiting. The dim light behind him throws half his face into shadow.

"Tes," he says, relief softening the roughness of his voice. He steps back to let me in.

I don't move. Instead, I hold out the folded paper. "What's this?"

He freezes. The muscles in his jaw work as he takes it from me, glances once, then tosses it onto the table without reading. "Where'd you get that?"

"In my locker." My voice trembles, but I keep it steady enough. "Is it true?"

For a long moment, silence stretches between us. His eyes flicker—anger, guilt, something unreadable. Finally, he says, "Yeah. It's true."

The admission hits me harder than denial. I'd braced for excuses. Not this blunt confession.

"Why didn't you tell me?" My voice cracks. "Why am I finding out from some anonymous note like I'm the last person who deserves the truth?"

He runs a hand through his hair, pacing like a caged animal. "Because it doesn't matter anymore. That was the past."

"It matters to me." My throat tightens. "You put someone in the hospital, Bran. That's not just a mistake. That's—"

"Violence?" He barks a laugh with no humor. "Like hockey isn't violence dressed up in jerseys and referees. Everyone loved it when I broke bones for the team. But the second it goes too far, suddenly I'm a monster."

"That boy almost died."

His steps falter. He looks at me, and for the first time, I see not anger but something rawer—fear, maybe. "I know." His voice is low, ragged. "I wanted him to."

The air leaves my lungs. "You—what?"

He presses his palms to his eyes like he wants to block out the world. "He taunted me. Called me trash. Said I'd never be more than the drunk's kid from Northbridge. And I snapped. For a second, all I wanted was to shut him up forever."

The confession chills me to my bones.

"I was suspended. Everyone hushed it up so scouts wouldn't bolt. Coach said it was a clean hit gone bad. My father called it the only thing I'd ever done right." He spits the words like venom.

I step back without meaning to. The wall brushes my shoulder blades.

"Tesni." His voice sharpens, desperate. "Don't look at me like that."

"How else am I supposed to look at you?" My pulse hammers in my ears. "You terrify me."

Something shatters in his expression. He crosses the room quickly, too quickly, and I flinch. He stops inches from me, hands hovering as if he wants to touch but doesn't dare.

"I scare myself too," he whispers. "Every day. But you—you make it stop. When you're around, the noise quiets. You're the only good thing left."

My heart aches despite the fear coiled tight in my gut. His words sound honest. Too honest.

I shake my head, trying to steady myself. "Wanting me to fix you isn't love, Bran. It's—"

"Don't say it." His hand slams against the door beside my head, the bang making me jump. The exit is blocked, his body a wall between me and the hall. "Don't you dare call it obsession. I can't lose you. Not you."

His nearness is suffocating. I can feel the heat of his body, the faint tremor in his arm where it braces against the door. His other hand hovers near my cheek, fingers curling and uncurling like he's fighting himself.

"You're scaring me," I manage, voice barely above a whisper.

Instantly, his hand drops, his face crumpling with guilt. "God, Tes, I'd never—" His voice breaks. "I didn't mean—"

The vulnerability undoes me. How can someone be both a menace and a wounded boy in the same breath?

"I just..." My voice cracks. "I don't know who you are. This sweet, protective guy—or the one in that article. The one who wanted blood."

"I'm both," he admits. "And I hate it. But I'd rather you know the ugliest parts of me than think I'm some hero. I'm not. I never will be."

Tears sting my eyes. "Then what are we doing?"

He leans closer, his forehead almost brushing mine. "We're surviving. We're clinging to the only thing that makes this life bearable. You."

My legs weaken under the weight of his words. Fear and longing war inside me, neither strong enough to win.

"Let me go," I whisper.

He shakes his head, desperation flashing. "Not until you understand. Not until you see that what I feel for you is real. That I need you more than air."

His hand trembles as it brushes my cheek—soft this time, reverent, like I might dissolve if he presses too hard.

"Please," he murmurs. "Don't walk away. Not when you've already seen the worst of me."

I should shove him aside. I should run. Instead, I stand frozen, caught between the urge to flee and the dangerous pull of his honesty.

His lips hover near mine, his breath warm against my skin. The tension coils tighter, unbearable, every nerve in my body alight with warning and want.

And I realize too late—I'm not moving away.

His lips brush mine before I can decide whether to stop him. It's not gentle—it never is—but it's not brutal either. Rough edges softened by hesitation. A kiss that feels like a question he's begging me to answer.

My mind screams that I should push him away, demand space, demand clarity. Instead, my body betrays me. My fingers curl into the front of his shirt, clutching the fabric like it's the only solid thing in a world tilting dangerously out of balance.

"Tesni," he breathes against my mouth, the sound of my name raw, broken. His forehead presses to mine as if he needs the anchor. "Tell me I haven't lost you."

"I don't know what we are," I whisper. The words are trembling, but I don't let go.

His thumb traces the line of my jaw, reverent. The storm in his eyes shifts—still dangerous, but tinged with something else. Something I can't name. "Then let me show you."

I should pull away. Instead, I let him guide me back toward the couch, his body crowding mine without quite touching. My pulse thunders, not knowing if it's dread or desire. Maybe both.

When he cages me in again, bracing himself against the wall, I'm not afraid—not entirely. There's fear, yes, but tangled with a thrill so sharp it feels like standing too close to fire. One wrong move and I'll burn.

And still, I don't step back.

His mouth crushes mine before I can think. There's no space to breathe, no space to resist, only his lips moving over mine with a hunger that makes my knees buckle. I should push him away. I should scream. Instead, I clutch at his shirt like I'll drown without him.

He groans, low and guttural, like the sound is being torn out of him. His hands grip my waist, rough, insistent, dragging me against him until there's nothing between us but heat and desperation. I gasp into his kiss, and he takes advantage, sliding his tongue past my lips, claiming me like I'm already his.

I want to tell him to stop. The word forms in my head but never makes it to my mouth. Because the truth is—I don't want to.

He pulls me backward, guiding me until the backs of my knees hit the couch. I fall with a soft thud, and he's on me instantly, braced above me, his weight pressing me into the cushions. His eyes search mine—stormy, desperate, pleading.

"Tesni," he rasps, voice raw. "Don't fight this. Don't fight me."

My chest heaves, torn between fear and the sharp ache of wanting. I should be terrified—and I am—but the terror coils with something darker, something I don't dare name.

His hand skims down my side, fingers brushing my ribs, my hip, until he finds the edge of my shirt. He lifts it slowly, deliberately, giving me every chance to protest. I don't. My arms lift of their own accord, letting him strip it over my head.

The shirt falls to the floor. His gaze drops to my skin, and the sound he makes is half-growl, half-prayer. He lowers his mouth to my collarbone, teeth scraping, tongue soothing, marking me in ways that feel permanent. My back arches, my fingers tangling in his hair, pulling him closer.

"You don't know what you do to me," he whispers against my skin, his breath hot and shaky. "You don't know how close I am to breaking."

He drags his hand lower, over my stomach, pausing at the waistband of my jeans. He hesitates—just long enough to make me tremble—then pops the button and slides the zipper down with aching slowness.

"Bran..." My voice is a plea and a warning all at once.

He freezes, eyes locking on mine, wide and desperate. "Tell me to stop," he says, voice cracking. "Tell me and I will."

But I don't. I can't.

Instead, I lift my hips, the smallest invitation, and that's all it takes. His control shatters. He yanks my jeans down, cursing under his breath, and his hand is on me, fingers pressing through thin fabric, finding heat and wetness that betrays every lie I could tell myself.

My gasp fills the air, sharp and helpless. He swallows it with another kiss, deep and bruising. His fingers slip beneath the barrier, stroking, claiming, coaxing sounds from me I don't recognize as mine. My body arches into him, chasing more, needing more.

He groans, forehead pressed to mine, sweat dampening his hair. "You feel that? That's me. That's us. No one else gets this."

I should run. Instead, I cling. My nails rake his back through his shirt, dragging him closer until there's no space left, no doubt left. Just him. Always him.

When he pushes my underwear aside and sinks his fingers inside me, I cry out, the sound sharp, unguarded. His eyes darken, hunger devouring restraint. He sets a rhythm that leaves me trembling, breathless, caught between panic and bliss.

"Mine," he murmurs against my throat, each thrust of his fingers punctuating the word. "Say it."

My lips part, but no sound comes. He curls his fingers just right, stealing my voice, stealing everything. My back bows, my vision blurs, and all I can do is hold on as the world narrows to his touch, his voice, his claim.

"Say it, Tesni," he demands again, rougher, desperate. "Say you're mine."

And when the climax rips through me, tearing me apart and remaking me in the same breath, I do.

"I'm yours," I gasp, broken and true.

The words undo him. He buries his face against my neck, shuddering, his whole body taut with restraint. I feel the tremor in his arms, the quake of barely leashed need. But he doesn't push further—not yet. Instead, he holds me tight, as if letting go would mean losing me forever.

"You don't get it," he whispers, voice shaking. "You just saved me. You don't even know."

I should feel terrified. But lying there, flushed and trembling beneath him, I feel only one thing.

Claimed.

14

Dark Discoveries

Branwen

The ribbon still lingers in my pocket, its threads frayed from the number of times I've turned it over in my hand. Black silk, delicate and deliberate.

I've replayed the scene a hundred times: Helena's coat, her pale hair flashing under the lamp, her graceful movements. The part of me that lives on instinct insists it was her. But instinct isn't proof, and proof is the only thing that will keep Tesni safe.

So, I hunt.

The first place I go is the library, because predators return to the scene of their triumph. The stacks are still and stale, only the rustle of pages and the scrape of chairs breaking the silence. I climb to the north wing where I'd seen the coat, my eyes tracing the scuffs on the floor. They're faint now, swept but not erased. Ghostly reminders.

A girl in round glasses looks up from her notes when she feels me watching. "Looking for something?" she asks, wary.

"Study group," I say, lying without pause. "Solaris. You seen her?"

She shakes her head. "Not today." Then, after a pause: "But there was a weird guy here earlier. Lurking near the tables."

My body tightens. "Describe him."

"Tall. Hood up. Didn't check out a single book. Just stood there until we noticed. Then he left."

It wasn't me. And if it wasn't me, then Tesni has another shadow.

I leave before the girl can ask questions.

Practice that afternoon is a blur. Hendricks yells, teammates shove, the puck rings off the boards. None of it matters. I keep seeing Tesni's face when she confronted me with the article, the way her voice shook, the way her eyes cut between fear and pity. I'd rather she screamed. Anything but that pity.

When practice ends, I don't shower. I throw my gear in a heap and bolt.

Night falls quick at UC Wisteria, swallowing the quads in ink. I slip through alleys behind dorms, my hood up, my ears tuned to every footstep. Tesni's study group meets Wednesdays in Carter Hall—three blocks off the main quad, in a lounge that smells like old coffee and chalk dust.

That's where I head.

Carter is a squat brick building, most of its windows dark. A single lamp glows in the lounge on the second floor. My chest eases when I see Tesni's silhouette inside—head bent, pencil moving.

I circle the building, staying in the shadows. The air tastes metallic, sharp. Then I see it: movement in the hedge near the side entrance. Someone crouched low, waiting.

My body goes taut.

The figure shifts, and I catch a glimpse of a backpack strap, a wrist pale against the dark. My pulse spikes. I'm halfway across the lawn when the figure slips inside the side door.

I sprint.

The hallway is narrow, fluorescent lights buzzing faint. I catch the smell before I see it—copper and rot.

The lounge door is ajar. I push it wider, muscles coiled for a fight.

And then I freeze.

She's sprawled on the carpet, one arm bent wrong, hair fanned across a pool of dark red. It takes a second to place her—her name flickers up from Tesni's stories. Mia, the girl who always brought highlighters in every color. The one who giggled through presentations, the one Tesni said had a nervous laugh but a kind heart.

Her eyes are glass now.

The world narrows to a pinpoint.

I crouch, my breath harsh. Her throat is cut—clean, efficient. Not an accident. Not a scuffle. Murder.

My gut twists. Tesni's study group. Tesni's circle.

This wasn't random.

"Fuck," I whisper, pressing my fists into the carpet.

For one crazy second, I think to call it in. Tell Hendricks, tell campus security. But the second passes. If I'm found here, crouched over a dead girl, they won't listen to words. They'll see my record. My temper. The boy in that article.

And they'll blame me.

I stagger back, my chest heaving.

Footsteps.

I slam myself into the shadow of the doorway as two students pass down the hall, laughing about something stupid, earbuds dangling. They don't look inside. Don't smell the iron. Don't see the crimson seeping across the carpet.

When their voices fade, I slip out the side door, my hands shaking. Cold air cuts through me like glass.

I should go straight to Tesni. Drag her out of Carter, away from danger. But what if whoever did this is still inside? What if they're watching her right now?

The thought claws at me.

I circle back, scanning windows. Through the lounge glass, I see Tesni still bent over her notebook, oblivious. She hasn't looked up. Hasn't noticed Mia missing.

My throat locks.

If she knew, she'd scream. And screaming would draw whoever left the body.

I make a decision.

I slip into the stairwell opposite the lounge and climb to the top landing, where I have a clean view through the glass. My back hits the cold cinderblock wall. I'll stay until she leaves. Until I know she's safe.

Every sound makes me twitch—the groan of pipes, the creak of doors. I grip the railing until my knuckles ache.

An hour passes. My phone buzzes: *Leaving now. Want to walk me back?*

Relief slams through me. I text back: *Already outside. Wait at the door.*

By the time she appears, sliding her arms into her coat, I've crossed the lawn. She looks up, surprised. "Bran? How long have you been—"

"Too long." My voice is rough. I tuck her close, scanning the dark edges of the quad. "Don't go to Carter alone again. Ever."

She frowns, confused. "What are you talking about? It's just study group."

Not anymore.

I want to tell her, but the words choke. If I say them, she'll ask why I didn't call anyone. Why I ran. Why my hands still shake.

So, I bite it down. "Just promise me," I say instead.

She studies me like she can read the storm inside. Then she nods slowly. "Okay. I promise."

It's not enough. Promises are paper. What she needs is walls, locks, a guard who never sleeps.

What she needs is me.

The next day I can't sit through class. Every squeak of the chalk, every shuffle of papers makes me want to scream. I skip Professor Hawthorne's lecture and stalk the halls instead, searching for Helena.

She's at the café with a cluster of friends, her laughter sharp as glass. But when her gaze flicks up and meets mine, something sparks there. Recognition.

I imagine her in the hedge, slipping into Carter. I imagine her blade flashing.

She tilts her head and smiles at me—slow, taunting.

My fists clench.

If I confront her here, in front of witnesses, I'll lose. If I drag her into the alley, I might find the truth. I almost move—almost.

Then Tesni's voice echoes in my head, soft and trembling: You terrify me.

I force my hands open. I walk away.

Sleep is impossible. Every time I close my eyes, I see Mia's face. The blood. The silence.

So, I roam.

Campus at two a.m. is a different animal—feral, restless. Lights hum, shadows twitch. Somewhere an owl hoots, low and haunting.

I circle the dorms, then the library, then Carter again. They've sealed the lounge with tape now, but no guards watch the door. Students whisper in corners, rumors blooming like mold: overdose, suicide, accident.

No one says murder. No one but me.

And I know, with a certainty that locks my bones, that Tesni is next if I don't stop it.

That morning, Hendricks corners me in the locker room. "You look like hell."

"Didn't sleep."

"Need to hear it from me?" His eyes narrow. "Something's wrong with you, Bran. You're skating reckless. Playing like you've got a death wish."

I shrug. He doesn't know how close to the truth that cuts.

"Sort it out," he warns. "Before you drag the whole team under."

I leave without answering.

By evening, I can't take it anymore. Watching isn't enough. Promises aren't enough.

So, I go to Tesni's dorm. She's surprised when she opens the door, hair mussed, books stacked high. "Bran? It's late."

"I need to be here," I say. My voice is hoarse. "Please. Just let me stay tonight."

She hesitates, torn between suspicion and softness. At last, she nods, stepping aside.

I sit in her chair while she studies, my eyes locked on the window. Every shadow beyond it feels like a threat. Every creak of the radiator feels like a warning.

I don't mention Mia. I don't tell her about Helena's smile, about the certainty building in my chest.

Instead, I whisper, "I'll keep you safe."

She doesn't hear. Or pretends not to.

But I mean it.

Even if keeping her safe means burning the world down around her.

15

Unmasking the Past

Tesni

The campus safety email arrives at 6:11 a.m.—"Incident in Carter Hall. Avoid area."—and says nothing that matters. By eight, yellow tape slices the doorway and rumor does the rest. Overdose, accident, prank gone wrong. No one says the word blooming under my ribs like a winter rose.

Murder.

Branwen left before dawn, a kiss at my temple, a command disguised as care: "Text me every hour." He watched my window all night. My phone buzzes now—You up? Where are you? Eat.—and I answer three clipped words before I go find Sophia.

She's at the Ivy Café with both hands around a paper cup. Her eyes are red. "Have you heard?"

"Only the email," I say. "Is it Mia?"

"They won't say." Her voice thins. "Nora texted at three. Paramedics. Blood." She looks away. "I was supposed to quiz her on Dickinson."

Mia's highlighters. Mia's laugh. Then a wall in my head.

Sophia's gaze holds. "Are you okay?"

"I don't know." I hear how small it sounds. "Bran stayed. He wants me to change routines."

"Wants," she repeats. "He stayed in your room?"

"On the chair," I say. "He's worried."

"He's controlling." She keeps her voice gentle. "And he's part of why you're isolated enough to miss the signs."

"He didn't do this." Reflex.

"I didn't say he did." She rests a hand on her laptop. "I'm begging you—look deeper. You told me about the article. Don't stop there."

Sophia opens the laptop; the blue light lifts against both our faces. "Name, hometown, high school," she says. "Local papers keep every-thing."

We search. Game recaps, a profile, a column about his slapshot. Then: "Northbridge High Incident Under Investigation." A bench-clearing brawl. One player hospitalized. No names; the comments do what the article won't: "Atthill." "Temper." "Coach cover."

My stomach tightens. "Follow-up," Sophia says.

"Temporary Restraining Order Filed by Local Teen." The preview is enough—first name Katie, "pattern of harassing behavior," docket num-ber visible. Sophia pivots to county records. There it is in bureaucratic font: Katie Jameson v. Branwen Atthill. Allegations: repeated messages, unin-vited appearances, threatening language. Order granted for six months.

We stare. The words sit between us like a third person.

"He was seventeen," I say, because a story needs a beginning. "Kids are stupid. She could have..." I stop before the word turns poisonous. "You weren't there," I add. "You didn't see him tell me he hates the part of himself that's like this."

"Hating isn't changing." Her kindness frays. "You are not rehab, Tes. Not an antidote. You're my friend. And you're teaching yourself to call hurricanes weather."

The cup in my palms feels too hot. "He isn't only bad," I say. "He's gentle with me."

"Two truths can fit in one person. But one of them still breaks bones." She closes the laptop. "I loved Mia. I love you. I can't pretend there's no pattern."

"I'm not pretending." The lie is that I can hold everything without spilling. "I'm trying to give him a future that isn't only his worst day."

"Then come to Detective Schultz with me."

Bran's last message glows: *Answer me. Please.* I slide the phone under my thigh.

"I can't," I say.

Sophia looks at me a long time. When she speaks, it's not angry, just tired. "Call me when you're ready to leave." She strokes my hair and goes.

I don't go to Schultz. I go to Professor Hawthorne.

His office smells like paper and sandalwood. Blinds half-closed comb the last light across the rug. He looks up from essays, concern already arranged on his face. "Tesni," he says. "Come in."

"I think Mia is dead." The word breaks at the edges.

His mouth tightens. "I heard there was an incident." He gestures toward the chair. "Please."

I sit and tell him almost everything: the tape, the rumors, Sophia's search, the order. Professor Hawthorne listens the way he does in seminar—quiet until the room empties itself.

"I don't know who I am in this story," I finish. "Saint, fool, caution."

"You're a student asked to manage more than any student should," he says. "And you're brave." He leans forward slightly. "I have worried about Mr. Atthill's influence. He is...charismatic. Volatile."

"He isn't only that," I say. "He's—"

"Complicated," Professor Hawthorne offers. "But complexity isn't absolution." He opens a thin book, taps a line. "We love to imagine ourselves the cure for the doomed." He glances up. "The doomed need consequences before they need cures."

I should bristle. I'm too tired. "What do I do?"

"First, boundaries. You change routines because you decide it, not because someone tells you. Leave if you feel unsafe; call if you're followed." He pours tea and hands me a cup; his fingers brush mine, a static thrum. "Second, let people whose job is safety do that job. If Detective Schultz reaches out, speak to him. If you want me present, I will be."

"What about school?" My voice is small.

"Then we give you permission not to think in perfect sentences." He smiles. "Extensions are possible." His hand rests a moment on the back of my chair. "You are not alone in this, Tesni. Call me anytime."

His steadiness feels like shelter and performance at once. I nod, say thank you, and mean it.

When I stand, so does he. In the narrow doorway, we are closer than I realize; the gold thread in his collar catches light. He steps back first. "Be careful walking," he says. "The dark starts early."

The quad is gray. Students cluster and murmur, eyes tugged toward Carter Hall. Frost rims the hellebore beds. I take the long way back, past the rink where "Despicable" bleeds into "Discopia," the bass a pulse in the brick.

My phone buzzes. *Where are you?* Then: *Answer me.* Then: *Please.*

I tell myself the please matters. Two truths: I am frightened and I am loved; he is dangerous and he is trying.

Leaving Professor Hawthorne's, I type. *Heading back.* I add, because I need it to be true as much as he does: *I'm not leaving you.*

A minute. Good, he sends. I'll meet you halfway.

I tuck the phone away and keep walking. Tape flutters where we used to laugh. Somewhere, a door slams.

Halfway across the quad, I see Sophia with her arm hooked through Nora's. I lift a hand I don't think she sees. My throat tightens. A rift is a river; you can ford it or learn its currents. Not tonight.

Bran appears where the path kinks toward the dorms, hood up, eyes scanning even as his mouth softens when he sees me. He reaches for my hand and I let him take it. His palm is cold; his grip is sure. We walk in step, and I tell myself that is what love is—a cadence you can match in the dark.

"I texted you," he says, almost light. "Twice."

"Office hours ran long," I say. "Professor Hawthorne gave me tea."

At the name, something tightens in his jaw, then smooths. "Good," he says, as if choosing the word. "Good." His thumb presses against the inside of my wrist, as if counting time. "You'll stay in tonight."

"I was going to," I say. "Because I want to."

He nods. We reach the hellebore bed by my dorm. A strand of black silk lifts in the wind, snagged on a stem. My breath catches. Bran plucks it free, winds it around his finger, and pockets it without comment.

"Come on," he says softly. "It's cold."

Inside, I set my phone on the desk and Bran sets his body between me and the window. I watch him, and I watch the space around him, and I watch myself watching, learning waves to know when to run.

Sophia's voice threads the quiet: *Call me when you're ready to leave.* Professor Hawthorne's voice answers: *Boundaries. Consequences.* Bran's voice is a lower current: *I'll keep you safe.*

Three currents in one room. I close my eyes and listen for which one is the tide.

Outside, the lamps hum. In the hellebore bed, something dark moves and is only wind. I tell myself I can hold two truths. I tell myself that will be enough.

16

Into the Abyss

Branwen

Detective Schultz's office feels more like a waiting trap than a room.

The blinds are half-drawn, slicing pale afternoon light into bands that cut across the desk. Dust floats lazily in the beams, at odds with the tension gnawing through my chest. The chair beneath me is hard, its arms deliberately too close together, the kind of thing designed to make you fidget.

Schultz doesn't sit right away. He prowls instead, big frame moving deliberately, the soles of his shoes squeaking against the tile. His reputation precedes him—a grinder of confessions, a man who's dragged out more truth than most suspects meant to part with.

"Mr. Atthill," he says finally, lowering into his chair with a heavy creak. His accent has that clipped Midwestern edge, steady as a metronome. "You and I need to have a very frank talk."

I lean back, arms folded, projecting the calm I don't feel. "Then talk."

He opens a manila folder with studied care, like he's unwrapping a gift. Inside: photographs. My gut clenches before I even register what they are. Mia from Tesni's study group—face pale, eyes closed, blood staining the collar of her blouse. The memory of stumbling across her body surges back sharp and metallic, like the taste of pennies in my mouth.

"You recognize her," Schultz observes.

"I found her," I say. "Behind the humanities building. I was just too scared to call it in."

"Right," he says, sliding the photo aside. "Well. It's interesting, isn't it? Young woman ends up dead, and who's first on the scene? Branwen Atthill." He fixes me with a gaze as heavy as a body check. "That kind of coincidence doesn't win you points."

"I'm telling you, I'm not the only one out there," I say, leaning forward. "Someone else has been following Tesni. Notes left in her books, gifts that aren't from me. You've got another stalker on your hands."

His eyebrows lift, amused. "Another stalker?"

"Yes." The word grates through my teeth. "You think I'd kill someone from her study group? What would that even get me?"

"Plenty," Schultz counters. He picks up a slip of paper from the folder. "Witnesses say you've been trailing Tesni Solaris around campus. Sitting in shadows while she studies. Showing up at her job. That doesn't look like protection, Mr. Atthill. It looks like obsession."

A heat climbs up my spine. "Witnesses. Who? Jenkins? Helena? They've had it out for me since day one."

"I don't disclose names at this stage," Schultz replies smoothly. "But I can tell you their statements line up. Independently. They describe a pattern. You watching her, inserting yourself into her space, showing up uninvited. Textbook stalking behavior."

My fists tighten in my lap. "You don't get it."

"Then help me get it." His tone sharpens, voice like a skate blade scraping the ice. "Because from where I sit, you look less like a concerned boyfriend and more like a suspect who can't control himself."

I bite down on the inside of my cheek until I taste blood. Control. That word gnaws at me. I want to snap back, to tell him how wrong he is, how

I'm the only thing standing between Tesni and whoever else is creeping in the dark. But the words knot in my throat.

"I didn't kill her," I manage finally.

"Maybe not." Schultz leans back, studying me. "But you've got a history, don't you? Fights on the ice. Trouble in high school. Restraining orders."

My breath stills. Tesni must have dug around. Or maybe he's just done his job too well. "Those were misunderstandings."

"Funny thing about misunderstandings," Schultz says, folding his hands. "They tend to pile up until someone ends up in the ground." He closes the folder with a snap. "You're on thin ice here, Atthill. Very thin. And if I were you, I'd think carefully about where you skate next."

He dismisses me with a glance toward the door. That's it. No cuffs, no formal charges. Just suspicion thick enough to drown in.

The cold hits me like a cross-check as I step outside the station. Breath fogs in the late-day air. My hands ache to hit something, someone. But I clamp down, force myself to move forward. Tesni. I need her. She'll understand. She always does.

By the time I make it across campus to her dorm, the sky's gone bruised purple. Students huddle in packs, laughter rising above the crunch of leaves underfoot. I ignore them all, pushing through until I'm standing at her door.

She opens before I can knock, as if she felt me coming. Her brown eyes widen, taking in my posture, my clenched jaw. "Branwen?"

"They think I did it," I blurt. The words tear out raw. "They think I killed her."

Tesni's hand flies to her mouth. "What?"

"Schultz had me in his office. He laid it all out. Witnesses, stories about me following you." I step inside, closing the door behind me, the small dorm room suddenly too tight for the storm inside me. "He thinks I'm obsessed with you."

Her face softens, her brows knitting. "Oh, Bran..."

I expect doubt. Expect fear. But what I see instead is something else entirely: compassion. That wide-open heart of hers, reckless in its generosity.

"I told him," I press, pacing the narrow strip of floor. "There's someone else, another stalker. I've seen signs. The notes, the gifts you didn't recognize. He didn't believe me."

Tesni steps closer, reaching for my arm. "Of course he wouldn't. Cops always want the simplest story."

I stop, stunned. "You believe me?"

"Of course I do." Her voice trembles but holds. "You've protected me from the beginning. You would never hurt me. You'd never hurt anyone close to me."

Her certainty sears through me, at once intoxicating and unbearable. I want to sink into it, to let it wash away Schultz's accusations, the witnesses' whispers. But it also makes something darker stir—the knowledge that her faith ties me tighter to her than chains ever could.

"You don't understand," I say, dragging a hand through my hair. "He had reports, Tes. High school fights. A restraining order from Katie Jameson. He made me sound like a monster."

Her hand cups my jaw, forcing my gaze back to hers. "That's the past. Everyone has a past. What matters is who you are now. With me."

I swallow hard, throat tight. "And who am I now?"

Her lips curve into a fragile smile. "You're the man I love. The man who needs someone to see the good in him."

The words lance through me. Love. She says it like it's fact, unshaken by Schultz's warnings, by the blood on my knuckles, by the storm swirling around us.

I want to believe her. I do. But another part of me snarls that love is just another word for possession. For keeping. For ensuring no one else ever gets close.

"Tesni," I murmur, pulling her against me. "You don't know what that means. Loving me. It's not safe."

"I decide what's safe," she whispers back. "And I decide you're worth it."

Her conviction shatters something inside me. For a heartbeat, I see two futures: one where I surrender to the light she insists is in me, and one where I sink deeper into the darkness that feels like home. Both futures have her at their center.

I press my forehead to hers, eyes squeezed shut. "I can't lose you."

"You won't." Her hands clutch at my shirt. "I'm not going anywhere."

The promise should ease me. Instead, it claws at the part of me that knows promises break, people leave, nothing lasts. I want to lock her away, keep her where no detective, no professor, no second stalker can reach.

My breath shudders out. Love or possession? Maybe they're the same thing.

Later, when she's asleep, curled against me, I lie awake staring at the ceiling—listening to the sound of the rain, which is falling, at last. Schultz's words echo, mixing with hers. Obsession. Love. Protection. Control.

I trace idle patterns on her back, each touch a vow and a warning all at once.

She believes I can change. She believes she can save me.

But deep down, I know the truth: salvation was never my game. Possession is.

And if the world thinks I'm guilty already, then maybe guilt is all I'll ever be.

17

Blind Faith

Tesni

The email comes first.

Campus Safety: Update on Carter Hall incident: foul play suspected. Investigation ongoing. Please exercise caution when walking alone at night.

"Foul play." They don't use the word murder, but everyone does anyway. The air hums with it—whispers in the café line, the rustle of gossip along library tables, text threads that light up at midnight with speculation.

And Branwen's name always hovers near the center, even when it isn't spoken.

By noon, the rumor hardens: Bran Atthill is the main suspect.

I hear it in the bathroom between classes—two girls I barely know, their voices echoing off tile.

"Schultz brought him in, I heard."

"Not surprised. He's been stalking that girl, Tesni, forever."

"You think she's in on it?"

I stumble out before they can notice me. My pulse roars in my ears. He didn't do this.

When I find him outside the rink, Branwen looks like the storm already found him. His knuckles are raw from practice, his hoodie dark with sweat, his eyes a shade too sharp.

"They're saying things," I blurt before he can speak. "That you're—the main suspect."

He exhales like it's no news at all. "Schultz told me." His jaw flexes. "They want it to be me. Easy story. Angry hockey player, bad history, wrong side of town."

The words land heavy. "But you didn't—"

"Of course not." His eyes snap to mine, fierce, almost wounded that I'd even form the thought. "You believe me?"

It isn't a question. It's a plea dressed as certainty.

"Yes." The word is immediate, instinctive. "I do."

Relief flashes across his face, chased by something darker—ownership, almost. His hand cups the back of my neck, thumb brushing the line of my hair. "You're the only one who does," he murmurs. "The only one who matters."

And just like that, my decision is made. He's innocent. He has to be.

***

Professor Hawthorne doesn't see it that way.

"Tesni," he says after seminar, when the others have filed out. His office smells faintly of cedar and tea. "May I have a word?"

I linger by the desk, hugging my notebook.

"I worry about you," he begins. "You've heard the talk. About Branwen."

"They're wrong." My voice cuts sharper than I intend.

"Are they?" He leans back in his chair, steepling his fingers. "Detective Schultz doesn't drag a student into interrogation without cause. And the evidence—"

"What evidence?" I snap. "Rumors? People who don't understand him?"

Professor Hawthorne studies me, his expression unreadable. "I understand him better than you think. Men who thrive on volatility often leave wreckage behind. They draw people in with intensity, make them feel singular, indispensable. It can be intoxicating. But dangerous."

Heat rises in my cheeks. "You don't know Bran. Not the way I do."

"Perhaps not," he concedes softly. "But I know patterns. And I know what it looks like when a bright, idealistic student is drawn into someone else's abyss."

His words land like stones. For a moment, I picture myself from the outside: following Bran, defending him, excusing him. The image flickers, and I shove it away.

"He needs me," I say. "And I need him."

Professor Hawthorne's sigh is heavy with resignation. "Need and love are not always the same."

I can't listen anymore. I leave before he can say another word.

That night, Branwen meets me by the hellebore beds. Frost has silvered the leaves, the flowers bowed like secrets under weight.

"They'll keep coming after me," he mutters. "Schultz, Hawthorne, half the damn campus. They all want me guilty."

"They don't matter," I insist, looping my arm through his. "I'm here. I believe you. That's enough."

He studies me, searching my face for cracks. Whatever he sees satisfies him. He exhales, shoulders loosening. "God, Tes, you're the only thing keeping me sane."

I rest my head against him, ignoring the voice inside that wonders if "sane" is a word that belongs here at all.

Still, Professor Hawthorne's warnings echo in my head.

Patterns. Intensity. Abyss.

I tell myself it's jealousy—he's seen me drift from his seminars, from the safe orbit of his mentorship. Maybe he resents Branwen for stealing my focus, for pulling me into a world where footnotes and essay drafts mean less than the pounding of skates on ice, the bruising grip of someone who sees me as essential.

And maybe I want it to be jealousy, because that means Branwen isn't the danger. The danger is outside. Helena's eyes flashing in lecture. The black silk ribbons that appear like omens. The sense of being watched even when Branwen's hand is clasped around mine.

I repeat it like prayer: The danger isn't Bran. The danger is out there.

The next morning, Schultz stands outside Carter Hall, clipboard in hand. Students swarm around him like anxious bees. He jots notes, asks questions, his eyes scanning faces.

When his gaze lands on me, something sharp flickers there. Suspicion, or pity—I can't tell. Branwen tenses at my side, shoulders squaring.

"Don't talk to him," Bran mutters. "He'll twist everything."

I nod, even as Schultz's stare lingers. My loyalty hardens into armor.

By week's end, the campus feels split in two.

Some students whisper that Branwen is violent, unstable, bound to break. Others, mostly teammates, insist he's being framed, a scapegoat for deeper rot.

And me? I walk the line between them, head high, hand in his. People stare. I let them.

Because this is what love looks like: standing firm when the world demands retreat.

Professor Hawthorne corners me again after class. His voice is lower this time, urgent.

"You may think I'm jealous," he says. "I'm not, though. I just care about your safety. Branwen is dangerous, Tesni. If not to others, then to you."

"He wouldn't hurt me." The certainty in my voice startles even me.

His expression softens, almost mournful. "That's what they all say. Until they're wrong."

The words follow me down the corridor like shadows.

That night, Branwen and I sit in his room, the silence thick. He traces the lines of my palm with his finger, slow, deliberate.

"They don't get it," he murmurs. "What we have. They think it's unhealthy, toxic. They want to pull you away."

"They won't," I promise.

He presses his lips to my wrist, right where the pulse beats. "Say it again."

"They won't pull me away."

"Good." His eyes burn into mine. "Because if I lost you..." His grip tightens. "I don't know what I'd do."

The words should scare me. Maybe they do. But they also spark something else—a dangerous thrill that I matter this much. That I'm not replaceable.

Blind faith, I think, and swallow the taste of the phrase.

The days blur, Schultz circling, Professor Hawthorne warning, whispers trailing behind me. Through it all, Branwen's presence is constant, heavy as gravity.

And I let myself believe that love is enough. That my faith can outweigh the shadows clinging to him.

Even as doubt scratches at the edges of my mind.

18

Twisted Revelations

Branwen

Schultz doesn't arrest me; he does something worse. He lets me go with the look of a man who's already written the ending.

Everyone looks, no one says my name aloud today.

I skate until the manager kills the lights. The ice keeps my secrets better than people do. Each lap burns a thought into white: Mia on the carpet. The black ribbon. Tesni saying yes when the world said no. Love, I think, and the word means oxygen and ownership at once.

On the path back I feel watched. Windows stare. A glint of pale hair slides out of sight. Helena—or the enemy my mind builds so I can be the shield.

I text Tesni: *North wing. Now.*

She answers: *Coming.*

After hours the library is lungs and hush. The north wing's glass wall shows the campus like an aquarium. I wait where the floor remembers a careful shoe.

Tesni slips in, tired and bright at once.

"They're saying—"

"I know."

"Tell me what to do," she says.

I could ask for anything. "Let me in," I say. "Past whatever keeps me an arm's length away."

"I'm here," she says, moving close enough that I feel her breath. "Then tell me what you haven't."

"You think confession is a neat box." I sink until we're eye level. "Fine. Hard truths." And I tell her everything.

Northbridge in winter: three rooms, broken heat, unbroken bottles. A father who taught me to leave marks and call it love. The first fight that felt like church. The cheer when a crowd scents blood and how it writes your pulse.

"I liked it," I say. "Not the win. The break."

She doesn't look away. "Hunger isn't a sin," she says quietly. "Biting the wrong thing is."

"Katie," I go on. "I said I'd stop showing up and didn't. I said I'd stop calling and didn't. I said I was proving something. She got the order. I learned the sound a door makes when the law stands behind it."

Tesni flinches, but keeps her palm on the shelf like she's bracing me up. "You were a kid."

"I'm still the same bones." I put my hand beside hers without touching. "And with you the wanting is worse. It feels like a room fills with water and the only way to breathe is with your mouth under mine. I need you close enough to count your breaths. Do you understand?"

"Yes," she whispers. I can't tell if it's answer or mercy.

"I didn't kill Mia," I say. "But if someone meant to hurt you, I don't know what I'd become on the way to stopping them." That is the truest thing in me.

She threads her fingers in my sleeve like she's anchoring both of us. "Thank you for telling me."

"You think a map cures a minefield," I say. "It doesn't."

"Maps keep people alive." She swallows. "What aren't you telling me?"

There's a camera on my desk I won't name, a blind corner I learned by counting steps, a ribbon I turn over when the world won't sit still. I choose silence; it tastes like iron.

"Nothing compared to this," I say.

She studies me too long; I look away first. Coward. "Then what do you need?" she asks.

I need to be the only fact in her day. I need rooms with no exits. "Proof," I say.

"Proof of what?"

"That you're with me. That this isn't just a story about saving someone broken." I tip my head toward the glass. Below, the common space waits—mostly empty, never abandoned. A librarian crosses sometimes like a slow comet. "Here," I say. "Where the world could see if it looked. Let the risk say what we can't."

She takes a diver's breath. "Why like this?"

"Because everything wants to take you." My voice is more force than sound. "Because I need to make a mark the night can't scrub out."

She closes her eyes. Opens them with a look that hurts. "Okay," she says. "I'm choosing this." She says it again, to herself. "I'm choosing."

"Say when," I murmur. "You say stop, it stops."

"Okay." She steps into me.

The first touch is not gentle. It never is. But I leash the part of me that breaks doorframes. My hands bracket her waist. Her mouth is warm and certain. Somewhere in the stacks, a cart clicks, far away. The thought of discovery slides through me like a blade dipped in sugar.

We move deeper into the shadow. The glass reflects us back as doubled ghosts. I back her into the column where metal meets stone and feel my own arms tremble. "Tell me again," I whisper against her mouth. "You choose this."

"I choose you," she says, fierce—as if the saying can build a wall. Her hands climb my shoulders, then my hair, and the claim undoes me.

The building settles; a vent hums. Down in the common, two freshmen chase a laugh, phone lights bobbing. They don't look up.

I nip the corner of her mouth—apology and demand. "If we're seen—"

"Then we're seen," she says, breathless, and I feel the decision settle in her spine.

The knot loosens, and with it words. "I think about you all the time," I say. "Not just the way you taste. The way you cut a paragraph until it bleeds right. The way you touch your sleeve before you tell the truth. The way you make a room quieter by standing in it." I press my forehead to hers. "I want to keep that room."

"Rooms aren't things you keep," she whispers.

"They are if I'm the door." Not a metaphor—a vow.

Her fingers find the hem of my hoodie. The world tightens to a square foot of air. I catch her wrist, not to stop, to memorize bone under skin. "You say when."

"I know." She kisses the small scar near my jaw, the one most people miss. "I'm not porcelain." Softer: "I'm afraid."

"So am I," I say, grateful for the truth. "Maybe that's the point."

Footsteps pass below, a cough, a door thuds. We still. My heart kicks like it wants out. I feel her fear and her want braided so tight they're one rope.

She rises on her toes, meets my mouth harder. The glass makes us a rumor. Risk tastes like salt.

"Tell me a secret you didn't put on the map," she murmurs.

I close my eyes. "I dream about locking the world out," I say. "The click of a deadbolt. Your keys in my pocket. Quiet that isn't empty because you're inside it." I don't say the other thing: counting her breaths by the shape of light under her window. "It scares me." That part is clean.

Her breath stutters. "Thank you." Gratitude hurts worse than judgment.

The cart squeaks again, closer. We flatten into the column's shadow, our bodies a language without tense. Her hands slip under my hoodie; heat runs my spine. The risk makes each inch electric. I tilt and taste the edge of her throat, her pulse a proof the world still moves.

A key turns. Lights shift. She bites her lip and presses her palm to my chest like a seal.

"Bran," she says—warning and want in one line.

"I've got you," I answer, and I do. If the world walks in, I'll take the blame and the blow and the fall. I'll take anything, as long as she keeps choosing me.

The corridor beyond the glass empties. The hush returns, deeper for being briefly broken. In it, we press closer, writing on each other the story we can't say out loud.

Outside, the hellebore beds hold frost like a secret. Inside, the night leans in to listen.

Tesni's breath hitches as I press her closer to the column, the glass wall throwing our reflections back at us. Her eyes flick nervously toward the empty corridor beyond, but she doesn't pull away. She stays.

"You said you choose this," I murmur, my mouth grazing the words against her skin.

"I do," she whispers, though her voice trembles. Her fingers twist in my hoodie, anchoring herself to me even as her body quivers between want and fear.

Every sound in the library sharpens—the creak of a vent, the faint squeal of a cart two floors down. Each one could expose us. The thought doesn't slow me; it feeds me. The risk burns through my veins, daring the world to notice, to try and take her from me.

"Then let them see," I tell her, my voice rough, almost breaking. "Let them know you're mine."

She closes her eyes, pressing her forehead to mine, as if blocking out the world. "Bran..."

The word is part warning, part surrender. My grip tightens at her waist, not to hurt, just to remind her I'm here, that I'm not letting go.

And she doesn't ask me to.

Her whisper hangs between us, fragile and fierce: "I do."

That's all I need.

I crush my mouth to hers, swallowing the tremor in her voice, demanding more until she gives it. Her lips part, uncertain at first, then hungry. I seize the moment, sliding my tongue against hers, not gentle, never gentle—claiming her in the shadow of glass where anyone could look up and see.

My hands roam down her sides, greedy, memorizing every curve through thin fabric. She shivers when I hook my fingers beneath her shirt and drag it up, baring skin to the cold air. My palms cup her breasts, thumbs brushing her nipples through lace. She gasps, the sound sharp in the hush, and the risk of being overheard makes me harder than I've ever been.

"You feel that?" I rasp, grinding against her thigh so she knows exactly what she's doing to me. "That's yours, Tesni. No one else gets this."

Her breath stutters. She looks toward the glass, toward the dim shapes passing below, then back at me with wide, blazing eyes. "Then take it," she whispers. "Take me."

The leash snaps. I spin her, pressing her front against the column, her palms flat against the cool stone. I press in from behind, my body a wall against hers. Her ass grinds back instinctively, and the friction rips a groan out of me.

I shove her skirt up, exposing pale skin that gleams in the low light. My fingers hook her panties, dragging them down her thighs. The sight nearly undoes me—her trembling legs, the perfect curve of her ass, the slick heat I find when I slide my fingers between her thighs.

She moans, soft and strangled, muffled against her own arm. I press harder, rubbing circles over her clit before thrusting two fingers inside her without warning. She cries out, jerking, but doesn't pull away. Her body yields, stretching around me, soaking my hand.

"God, Tes," I growl into her ear, pumping my fingers in and out, harder, faster, until her hips chase me. "You're dripping for me. For me."

She gasps, her nails scraping the stone, her voice breaking. "Someone—someone might see—"

"Let them." I bite her shoulder through her shirt, marking her. "Let them know who you belong to."

Her legs shake, her whole body taut with the effort to keep quiet. I pull my fingers out, slick with her arousal, and she whimpers at the loss. That sound nearly wrecks me. I free myself, stroking my cock once before pressing the tip against her wet, swollen entrance.

"Say it," I demand, my voice low and shaking with need. "Say you choose me."

"I choose you," she gasps, desperate, clutching the column like it's the only thing keeping her upright.

That's all. I slam into her in one brutal thrust, burying myself to the hilt. Her cry echoes off the stone, loud enough to make us both freeze for a heartbeat—but no footsteps come. The silence swallows us again.

I don't stop. I can't. I pound into her, each thrust hard enough to rattle the glass at our backs. Her body tightens, gripping me like a fist, every squeeze pulling me closer to the edge.

"Bran," she moans, her voice raw, pleading.

"That's it," I snarl against her ear, slamming harder, deeper. "Take me. Take all of me."

Her hips push back, meeting me stroke for stroke, reckless, fearless now. The sound of our bodies colliding fills the wing, obscene and perfect. My hand fists in her hair, yanking her head back so I can bite her throat, leaving marks that will outlast tonight.

She shatters first, her whole body convulsing around me, clenching so hard I nearly lose it. Her cry tears through the hush, muffled only by my hand clamping over her mouth at the last second. She's writhing, pulsing, milking me until I can't hold back any longer.

I drive into her once, twice, three more times before spilling into her with a guttural groan, my vision going white. I hold her pinned, grinding until every drop is buried deep inside her, until she's shaking, boneless against the column.

Slowly, I ease out, tugging her skirt back down, pulling her into my chest before she can crumble to the floor. She trembles against me, her breath ragged, her lips parting like she wants to speak but can't find words.

I kiss her temple, softer now, reverent. "You're mine," I whisper. "Even if the whole world's watching, you're mine."

Her eyes meet mine, dazed and shining. She doesn't argue. She doesn't run. She just leans into me, and that's proof enough.

19

Choices and Consequences

Tesni

The silence between Sophia and me is louder than shouting.

When I pass her in the quad, she looks through me like I'm glass. Her arm is looped through Nora's, her hair pulled back in the messy knot she always wears when she's stressed. I almost say her name, almost break the ice with some small thing—class notes, coffee plans, anything. But her gaze slides past me, cool and deliberate, and my throat closes.

She warned me. I didn't listen.

Now Mia is gone, Branwen is accused, and Sophia won't speak to me.

I tuck deeper into my coat and keep walking. The air is sharp with the scent of frost and damp leaves, the campus shrinking into winter. Students gather in clusters, whispering about Carter Hall, about detectives, about the hockey star who's too violent for his own good.

Their eyes follow me, and I imagine what they're saying: She's the one. She's with him.

At the corner near the library, I run into Helena. Literally—she rounds the column at the same time, and our shoulders bump.

"Oh." She steadies herself, then smirks. "Tesni."

Her voice drips with false sweetness. Today she's wrapped in a sleek black coat, her blonde hair falling in practiced waves. Even in the cold, her makeup is flawless.

"You look tired," she says, eyes glinting. "Not sleeping well?"

I force my lips into a neutral line. "Excuse me."

But she steps sideways, blocking my path. "You must be under so much pressure. Everyone watching, everyone wondering if you're safe. Or if you're just naïve." She tilts her head, feigning sympathy. "It must be exhausting, defending someone no one else believes in."

Her words hit sharper than they should. I want to walk away, but my feet root. "You don't know him."

"Oh, I know enough." Her smile widens. "Branwen Atthill is a storm, and storms don't change just because you wish them to." She leans closer, her perfume sharp and cloying. "Careful, Tesni. Standing too close gets people hurt."

I push past her before she can see the heat in my eyes...or the tremor in my hands.

The rink is my refuge.

Cold air, sharp light, the scrape of blades against ice. I sit on the metal bleachers, my breath puffing in white clouds, and watch Branwen circle like a predator on the hunt. Every stride is power, every pivot sharp enough to cut. He doesn't notice me at first. His focus is absolute.

Hendricks paces at the boards, arms folded, shouting instructions. The team runs drills, passes sharp, pucks slamming into nets. Branwen moves like he's trying to outrun something, or someone.

When the whistle blows and practice breaks, Hendricks finally notices me. He jogs up the steps, his expression a careful mask.

"Tesni." He sits a row below me, pulling off his gloves. "You here for him?"

I nod.

"You care about him," he says flatly. Not a question.

"Yes."

He exhales, running a hand through his hair. "He's a hell of a player. Fierce. The kind of guy who can turn a game on its head. But off the ice..." Hendricks shakes his head. "I've seen where that intensity leads."

I swallow hard. "He's not what people say."

"Maybe not. But he's not what you think, either." Hendricks looks me square in the eye. "He plays to dominate, not just win. That doesn't switch off when the skates come off. You know that, right?"

My chest tightens.

"He's had close calls. Fights. Suspension in high school. Every time, people made excuses—'boys will be boys,' 'heat of the moment,' 'bad background.' But excuses don't erase patterns." Hendricks leans forward, elbows on knees. "I'm not telling you to leave him. That's your decision. I'm telling you to stop pretending the red flags are green."

The words cut deep because they echo what I've already heard from Sophia, from Professor Hawthorne, from Schultz in his blunt interrogation notes. And still, my instinct is to shield Branwen.

"You don't know him like I do," I whisper, hating how small my voice sounds.

Hendricks doesn't flinch. "Maybe I don't. But I know what obsession looks like when it eats a man alive. And I see that in him. So, be honest with yourself, Tesni—are you helping him, or are you drowning with him?"

That night, Branwen walks me home, his hand heavy on my back. His presence is both comfort and cage.

"They're still looking at me," he mutters. "Like they're waiting for me to break."

"They don't matter," I say automatically, though Hendricks's words replay in my head. Obsession eating a man alive.

He stops beneath the hellebore beds, frost sparkling under the lamps. "Do you believe me?" His voice is low, urgent.

"Yes." The answer comes too fast. Too easy.

But the certainty I once carried is starting to crack. Images flash behind my eyes: Branwen's fists clenched, his temper flaring, his confession that he wanted to kill a boy once. The way he held me in the library, daring the world to see.

And still, I can't say no to him. I can't walk away.

Because what if everyone else is wrong? What if love really can change him, heal him? What if I'm the only one willing to stay when no one else will?

The questions twist around each other like ivy, suffocating but familiar.

Back in my dorm, I sit at my desk long after he's gone. My phone is filled with unread messages from Sophia—weeks old now, frozen in time. My notes lie scattered across the desk, a half-finished essay abandoned beside the article about Branwen's fight in high school. The headlines blur together: Violence. Restraining order. Dangerous.

I close my eyes, pressing my palms to my temples.

If I leave him, I abandon him to the darkness everyone claims he belongs to. If I stay, I risk becoming collateral damage in his storm.

It's not the fairytale I grew up believing in. But maybe fairytales were always lies. Maybe love is supposed to be messy, terrifying, destructive. Maybe that's what makes it real.

The next morning, I catch sight of Helena again across the quad. She's laughing with friends, but her gaze flicks to me and lingers, sharp as a blade.

Something coils in my stomach. Branwen is not the only danger circling me.

And yet, when I think of who I'll walk beside, who I'll hold onto in this storm, my heart still chooses him.

Even as the cracks in my certainty widen.

20

Collision Course

Branwen

Doubt is a small thing in her voice—just a hairline crack—but I hear it the way a defenseman hears a bad edge on his blade.

A weakness. A place where the ice will give.

Hendricks got to her. Professor Hawthorne keeps circling. Schultz watches me like he knows I won't choose the right door if there are two.

So, I make sure there's only one.

The campus turns thin at dusk, lanterns coughing halos over the hellebore beds, windows breathing yellow. I walk the same routes the patrols walk until I know the seams—where the security cameras blink, where the pathlights die, where the custodial doors don't latch if you lift and push.

Her dorm has a blind spot two doors down from the north entrance. The hinge that screams if you don't catch it. The service stair that smells like lemon and old dust. I've counted the steps, timed the sweep of the lobby camera, learned the delay on the motion sensor that lights the second-floor landing. If the world won't protect her, I will. If the world tries to take her, I'll break its fingers.

The first note is a pressed hellebore with black silk. I studied Helena's knots until I could make the ribbon lie the way hers did—expensive, soft as breath. On the card, I print a hand I don't recognize: uneven script, tilted to the left, the kind of writing that says you learned your letters late. I write: "keep your light safe."

I leave it in Tesni's desk drawer under her highlighters.

The second note slides behind her mirror so it winks at her when she tilts it to pin up her hair: "the night is watching." I add no flower this time. Too much sugar and the teeth don't ache; you have to vary the dose.

The third is a whisper folded into a book she's reading. I know which book because I watch what she carries and I remember the shape the way other people remember faces. The card says: "you weren't alone last night."

It's not a lie.

Every note lands without landing on me. She texts: *another ribbon. i hate it.* Then: *Report?* But she deletes that. She's learning my language. We never name the police. We name danger like a person we can grab by the throat.

I hold the ribbon in my pocket until the silk warms and forgets what it was tied to.

For the second part, I need a ghost with legs.

Evan's taping his stick when I slide onto the bench beside him after practice. We're alone—the others drifted toward showers, the whine of hair dryers already starting in the tile echo.

He's the kind of boy who likes the sound of his own speed, not the sound of hard questions. Blond, broad, stubborn. Good at not thinking until the thinking's done for him.

"We're going to take a walk," I tell him.

He smirks without looking up. "Got plans."

"You had plans the night you and Danilo turned Discopia's back hallway into a boxing ring." I keep my voice light. "Security cams love guys who throw punches under the blue lights."

His tape halts. "What?"

"The bouncer's my cousin." It's a lie, but it fits, and lies work best when they fit like borrowed coats. "He sent me clips. Be a shame if Hendricks saw them. Be a shame if Schultz got a copy. Be a shame if your scholarship learned you like to put your hands where they shouldn't go."

Evan swallows. He knows better than to ask how I know who he threw fists with, how I got the time stamp right. I know things because I stand where no one looks, and I listen until details show up dressed as themselves.

"What do you want?" he says, slow, like he's stepping onto ice he doesn't trust.

"Easy," I say. "You put on a mask. You follow a girl from the library to the hellebore path. You don't touch her. You don't speak. You walk like someone who isn't sure they can stop themselves. And when I arrive, you run."

"Jesus, Bran."

"No Jesus," I say. "Just a favor you'll be glad you did when your coach keeps coaching you and the detective keeps not knowing your name."

He stares at me, jaw working. "You're not right, man."

"Maybe not," I say. "Maybe I'm the only thing that is."

He hates me for a full ten seconds, then he nods because hate without leverage is just air. I toss him the mask—a cheap black neoprene thing with no logo—and a baseball cap to shade his eyes. He catches them on reflex.

"You don't touch her," I say again, flat. "If you do, I'll break your wrist in three places and call it a fall in the locker room. No one will ask me twice."

He believes me. He should.

I map the night like a coach maps a play.

Tesni's study group is at the library from eight to ten. She always lingers to copy a passage neatly after everyone leaves; her hand goes steadier when she writes for herself. She has tells—touching her sleeve before she says something true, rubbing the corner of a page before she turns it. The tells tell me when to position, when to wait.

I put Evan in the east stairwell at 9:50. I take the north stairwell at 9:55. I slip the fourth note into Tesni's satchel at 9:58 so she'll find it on the path, so the danger becomes present tense without my having to say it.

"do you feel me yet," the card says.

I hate the card. I hate that I want it to work.

At 10:03 she leaves the library, brown coat, hair tucked poorly into her scarf, the way she does when she's been thinking too hard to remember herself. She texts me out of habit: *heading back.*

On the path, the lamps hum and toss moth-snow in their halos. The hellebore beds are black fans under frost. The note finds her hand because I planned the place it would fall.

She reads. Her shoulders go rigid. She looks left. Right. The night is a throat about to swallow.

Evan steps out of the hedge in the mask and cap, hands empty, posture all wrong—too much football, not enough shadow. I feel a sliver of anger because detail matters and because fear ought to look like ballet when you do it right.

She hears him before she sees him, that soft scrape of a shoe, and then she does see him and the breath she makes isn't quite a sound. She moves fast—quicker than I've watched her move toward anything but a new idea. Toward the hellebore path, toward the blind angle where the lamp skips and the camera blinks, and I wait like a hunter behind a tree that looks like any tree to anyone who hasn't loved it for hours.

"Hey," Evan says without thinking, and I wish I'd taped his mouth instead of his stick. He catches himself, swallows the word, makes his silence menacing. I'll teach him silence if he lives long enough to need it.

Tesni breaks into a run. Evan follows because the script says follow.

I step into the path when they hit the dark patch.

The collision is a chapter I know by memory: shoulders low, center of gravity under his, my forearm a bar across his chest, the twist that dumps him sideways without breaking his fall. It reads like protection and feels like possession and I let it.

Evan hits dirt, lets out a grunt he doesn't have to fake. I pin him with a knee to the hip and a hand on the mask, slam his head once—not hard, just enough to ring. He'll have a headache. He'll learn not to be sloppy.

"Get the hell away from her," I snarl, voice not performative because I mean it in ways that don't need performance. To Evan, I whisper so only he hears, "Run."

He runs. He's good at that part.

Tesni's back hits the brick, hands up like she's bracing for the building to tip. Her eyes are enormous, dark blown wide, and I hate myself for liking the way she looks at me when I'm the only thing standing between her and a shape with teeth.

"I've got you," I say, already moving to her, already making my body into a wall she can choose not to lean on. She leans anyway. She shakes. I feel it through both our coats.

"What—" Her voice splinters. "Did you see his face?"

"No." I keep my voice low. Steady. "Mask. He was sloppy. He ran."

"We should call—" She doesn't finish the noun. She's learned. Or I've taught her.

"Not here," I say. "Not yet. He's gone. You're okay." I say it until the words feel like the kind of lie the body believes because it wants to. "Can you walk?"

She nods, the nod of someone whose spine is acting on her behalf while her mind catches up. I keep my hand on her back, light pressure. The winter air tastes like pennies and breath.

We move toward the brighter path. Students drift in pairs, oblivious. The lamps buzz. The hellebore bed holds its frost like a secret it won't share.

And then I feel it more than see it—the way a gaze can be a hand on your collar from across a parking lot.

Schultz stands under a dead lamp at the far side of the quad, bulk in a dark coat, hat pulled down. He doesn't make the mistake of standing under light; he lets the light make a silhouette of him anyway. His posture says patience. His face is shadow. The ember of a cigarette writes a red comma in the dark when he lifts it.

He's close enough to see the mask in my hand if I were dumb enough to still be holding it. He's far enough that he didn't see me lay a boy on the ground and tell him to run. He's exactly the distance of a man who likes to watch without interrupting the experiment.

Our eyes meet through the dark the way predators recognize each other at a water hole: not friends, not strangers.

If he lifts a hand, it's not a wave. It's an acknowledgment. It says: I see what you're doing even if I don't know how you did it. It says: keep skating on this ice and one day it will crack and I will be right there with a rope I won't throw in time.

Tesni doesn't see him. Or if she does, she thinks he's a tree, a statue, another man waiting to be something.

"Let's get you inside," I say, voice a notch lower so it won't carry. I angle my body so she can't turn her head the way her body wants to, the way curiosity pulls. I don't need Schultz's eyes on her. I don't need his patience to bend toward her name.

In the lobby's fluorescents, her face is too pale. The RA at the desk looks up, clocks the shake in her hands, the way I stand like a door, and decides to look down again. People like doors when they point in the direction they were already walking.

"Do you want water?" I ask.

She nods. I get it for her. She drinks the way you breathe after almost drowning—greedy, then ashamed of the greed.

"Do you want me to stay?" I ask, and the truth is I barely manage the question mark. Want and need are bare wires in me. I'm careful which ones I touch when she's looking.

"Yes," she says, small. "Just...sit. Please."

We go to her room. The notes I placed might as well burn through the walls. I take the chair. I do the thing Hendricks would recognize as stillness and Schultz would call staging. Sometimes the only way to look harmless is to remind your body how to be a piece of furniture.

She sits on the bed with her knees up and the water in both hands like it needs human heat to keep from spilling. After a time, the shaking fades. When she finally looks at me, the gratitude hurts more than suspicion would have. Gratitude is a leash I would choose to wear.

"You saved me," she says, and I hate that she's right.

"I was close," I say. Not a lie. I plan to be.

"I keep thinking about his hands," she whispers. "Empty. But I thought—" She doesn't say the word knife. We don't need it.

"There are worse things than empty hands," I say. I'm one of them. I make my voice softer. "You're safe now."

She nods. Her eyes flick to the window, then to me. "Stay," she says again, almost apologizing for the ask. "Just tonight."

"Yeah," I say. "Just tonight." The word just rolls around the room like a coin you can't catch under the radiator. It will be there in the morning, too.

She curls down into her pillow while I take up the work of watching. Somewhere between a blink and the next, her breath finds its rhythm. I count without meaning to. When she stirs, I'm already on my feet and I hate that I move before knowing why.

In the sliver of glass between the shade and the window frame, the quad is a geometry of dark. The place where Schultz stood is empty. If he was ever there, he's gone to write the story he thinks he's seeing. Or to wait where the story will trip on its own laces.

I press my palm to the glass until the cold tells me I'm still here. My reflection looks like a man in a tank ready to empty.

You made her need you, a voice says.

I made her safe, another answers.

Both are true. Only one feels like love. The other feels like winning.

I sit back down. The ribbon in my pocket has warmed to my skin. I don't take it out. I already know what it looks like.

Tomorrow there will be more whispers. Evan will avoid my eyes and keep his wrist. Schultz will stand in a new shadow with the same patience.

Hendricks will tell me to get my head right or stay off his ice. Helena will glide near a doorway and let the silk of her coat say a thing her mouth won't.

Tesni will look at me like I'm oxygen. I will make sure there's no other air.

The ice groans somewhere in my memory, a sound that means change or break. I close my eyes and listen for which one it is.

21

Crossroads

Tesni

The dorm room feels too small, too quiet, as I wait for him. My books are scattered across the desk, but I haven't read a single page. All I can hear is the hollow echo of Detective Schultz's voice from last night, warning questions cloaked in politeness, and Branwen's arm around me as if nothing had happened. My chest tightens just remembering the way he said he would always protect me — protect me from what, though? Or who?

The knock comes, sharp, impatient. I know it's him before I move.

When I open the door, Branwen fills the frame. His hair is damp from practice, his eyes lit with that electric blue intensity that's equal parts comfort and threat. He pushes inside without asking, and suddenly the air feels too dense, charged.

"We need to talk," I say quickly, before he can derail me with a kiss.

His jaw flexes. "About what?"

"You know what." My voice wavers, but I hold his gaze. "The notes. The...rescue. All of it. Bran. It's all just so much."

For a heartbeat, he's motionless. Then he shuts the door with a quiet finality that makes my stomach lurch.

"You want the truth?" His laugh is low, bitter. "Truth is, I don't sleep. Haven't, not really, since I was a kid. My old man made sure of that. You never knew when he'd come crashing through the door, fists first, questions never. My mom? She left years before that. So yeah, I learned to fight early. Learned that if you want something to stay yours, you hold on with both hands. You don't let go, no matter who tries to rip it away."

The words tumble out of him, harsh and raw. I've never heard him talk like this, never seen his armor crack so wide.

"Bran..." I whisper.

He shakes his head, pacing like a caged animal. "You think I don't know what they say about me? The monster on the ice. The psycho who put Davis in the hospital. They're right. I am that guy. Violence is the only language I learned, and it's the only thing that ever gave me control. Until you."

His eyes snap to mine, wild and pleading all at once. "You don't understand what you are to me, Tesni. You're not just light, you're oxygen. And I don't care if that makes me obsessed or dangerous. I'll burn this whole campus to the ground before I lose you."

The confession hits me like a blow, but instead of fear, what I feel is a wave of fierce, aching compassion. The boy behind the mask — broken, battered, clawing for love in the only way he knows how. My chest tightens with the certainty that this is my moment, the moment I've been waiting for.

I step closer, reaching up to touch his face. "You don't have to burn anything. You don't have to fight the world anymore. Not with me. You don't need to control everything to be loved."

His breath shudders out, and for the first time, his shoulders slump, like the weight he's carried forever is too much. "You think you can fix me? Patch up what's already ruined?"

"I don't want to fix you." My voice trembles, but I press on. "I want to love you. All of you. The parts that scare everyone else. The parts that scare even you."

He stares at me, searching for the lie. When he doesn't find it, something in him breaks. He surges forward, hands gripping my arms, rough, desperate. His mouth crashes onto mine — not gentle, not careful, but starving. The force of it slams me back against the wall, stealing my breath.

For a moment, I think about pulling away, about reminding him I wanted to talk. But my body betrays me, arching into him, answering with equal urgency. It's messy, bruising, more fight than kiss. And yet it feels like the truest conversation we've ever had.

His fingers tangle in my hair, his body pinning mine, his heart pounding against my chest. I clutch at him like he might vanish, like if I let go, he'll retreat behind the walls again. Every sharp edge of him presses into me, and I welcome it, needing to feel how real he is, how alive we both are in this fevered collision.

We stumble toward the bed, tangled and breathless, our mouths never parting for long. His hand finds mine, pinning it above my head as he hovers over me. His gaze is fierce, unblinking. "Say it," he growls. "Say you're mine."

"I'm yours," I whisper, not because he commands it, but because in this moment it feels true. It feels inevitable.

The fire in his eyes flickers into something softer, almost broken. He kisses me again, slower now, reverent, as if he's afraid I'll disappear if he blinks. Our bodies mold together, moving in rhythm, the world narrowing until there is only the heat of him, the press of his chest, the rough slide of his hands. Nothing explicit, but everything implied — the desperation, the surrender, the illusion of safety.

I think of all the stories I grew up on — the tortured heroes, the doomed romances. I always told myself I wanted something real, something lasting. But maybe this is what love actually looks like: messy, frightening, overwhelming, a fire you can't control.

As he buries his face in my neck, murmuring that he needs me, that I've saved him, I let myself believe it. I let myself believe I've finally broken through the walls of ice and rage, that he's letting me see the boy beneath the monster.

The bed creaks as he lowers me onto it, his body hovering above mine, heat radiating through his damp shirt. My heart slams against my ribs, every nerve alight with need. His mouth finds mine again, not as rough this time but still urgent, like he's starving and I'm the only thing that can feed him.

I fist my hands in his shirt, pulling him closer until the weight of him pins me to the mattress. His kiss deepens, tongue stroking mine, hungry and raw. Each brush of his lips feels like a vow, each breath a confession he can't say out loud.

"Tesni," he murmurs, the sound breaking apart in his throat. His fingers slip under my sweater, pushing it up slowly, reverently. The brush of his knuckles across my stomach makes me shiver.

I lift my arms, and he strips it off, tossing it aside. His gaze sweeps over me, drinking me in like I'm something holy. The fire in his eyes softens to something that makes my chest ache.

"You're beautiful," he says, like the words hurt to speak.

Heat floods me. "Show me," I whisper.

He obeys without hesitation, bending to kiss the swell of my breast through the lace of my bra. His lips trace the edge, then his teeth catch the strap, pulling it down until his hand can take over. When his mouth closes around me, hot and insistent, I cry out, clutching at his hair. He sucks gently at first, then harder, each flick of his tongue unraveling me further.

I can't think, can't breathe. I arch against him, desperate for more.

He groans against my skin, sliding lower, kissing down my stomach until he reaches the waistband of my jeans. His fingers fumble with the button, then tear it open. He looks up at me, eyes blazing. "Stop me if you don't want this."

The words shake something loose inside me. "I want you," I whisper, fierce, certain.

That's all he needs. He drags my jeans down in one rough motion, leaving me bare but for the thin scrap of lace between us. His hand cups me there, pressing, teasing, and I jolt, a cry escaping before I can stop it. He grins against my thigh, wicked and reverent all at once.

"You're already wet," he says hoarsely, slipping his fingers under the fabric, finding me slick and ready. "For me."

"Yes," I gasp, hips rocking into his hand.

He pushes the lace aside and slides his tongue against me. The first stroke is tentative, as if he's savoring, but the second is greedy, confident. My head falls back, a strangled moan tearing free as he uses his tongue masterfully, stroking, circling, driving me higher with every pass.

My hands clutch the sheets, then his hair, pulling him closer, desperate for more. He groans into me, the sound vibrating through my core. His fingers slide inside at the same time his tongue presses harder, and the combination shatters me.

"Branwen—" His name rips from my throat, helpless.

"That's it," he growls against me, voice muffled but triumphant. "Say my name when you come."

I do. The orgasm slams through me, fierce and unstoppable, my body arching off the bed as wave after wave crashes over me. My nails dig into his shoulders, and he holds me down, riding me through every spasm until I collapse, trembling, gasping.

Before I can catch my breath, he's crawling up my body, kissing me hard, letting me taste myself on his lips. He fumbles with his own jeans, shoving them down. His cock presses hot and hard against my thigh, and the hunger in his eyes leaves no question.

"I need to be inside you," he rasps, forehead pressed to mine. "Now."

I nod, breathless. "Yes. Please."

He thrusts into me in one long, deep stroke, filling me completely. I gasp, clinging to him as he stills, his whole body shaking with restraint.

"God, Tesni," he groans, burying his face in my neck. "You're perfect."

Then he moves, slow at first, each roll of his hips drawing me open, making me whimper. He kisses me again, softer now, every thrust deeper, more deliberate. The heat builds fast, our bodies finding a rhythm that feels inevitable, unstoppable.

I wrap my legs around him, pulling him closer, needing all of him. He pounds harder, faster, and the bed rattles beneath us, our breaths coming ragged and desperate.

"I love you," he gasps, the words torn out of him like they've been caged too long.

Tears sting my eyes. "I love you too," I whisper, and I mean it, every fractured, dangerous piece of it.

His thrusts grow erratic, his breath hot against my ear. "Come with me," he pleads. "Please, Tesni—now."

And I do. We do. We fall together, hard and fast, the world shattering around us. My cry mixes with his groan as we convulse in unison, bodies locked, souls colliding.

When it's over, he collapses against me, chest heaving, sweat-damp hair falling into his eyes. I hold him close, my hand on the back of his neck, anchoring him.

He kisses me again, slow and tender now, nothing like the storm before. "You're mine," he whispers, voice breaking.

I press my lips to his temple. "Always," I whisper back.

And in that moment, I believe it.

22

The Tipping Point

Branwen

She said she'd never leave.

The words still ring in my head when I wake, raw and holy. She whispered them against my chest, her voice catching, her lips warm. I felt them sink into me like nails holding a house together.

I look at her sleeping now—hair spilling across the pillow, lips parted, her hand curled against my ribs—and the world almost feels quiet. Almost.

The noise never truly leaves. But when I look at her, I can believe in silence.

On the ice, I play like I own the rink. Hendricks shouts from the boards, but the sound can't reach me. Every stride is a victory lap. Every puck I slam into the net is proof.

She said always.

Teammates slap my back after a scrimmage. Evan won't meet my eyes, still haunted by the night in the path, but the others feed off my fire. They think it's momentum. They don't see that it's mania.

I see threats in every shadow of the stands. A girl with a phone out, recording. A group of guys laughing, maybe at me. A professor walking by the glass, his eyes lingering on Tesni's shape where she waits in the corner with her books.

Professor Hawthorne.

He hovers too close in class, his tone too warm when he says her name. He disguises it as mentorship, but I see through the mask. I know hunger when I hear it.

One afternoon, I slip into the back row and watch her take notes, her pen steady, her brow furrowed. Hawthorne circles the seminar table like he owns it.

"Excellent point, Tesni," he says, voice pitched lower than it should be. His gaze lingers just a moment too long.

I want to tear his throat out.

After class, I take her hand before he can. He pauses, watching, something unreadable in his expression. Maybe curiosity. Maybe envy. I glare at him until he looks away.

"Don't talk to him alone," I tell her when we're outside.

She frowns. "He's just my professor, Bran."

"Professors cross lines." I hear the edge in my voice and don't blunt it. "Promise me."

She squeezes my hand. "Okay. I promise."

But later that night, I imagine her in his office, the door shut, his voice soft. The image makes me clench my fists until my knuckles ache.

I start controlling the variables.

Tesni doesn't walk home alone; I'm always there. If she wants coffee, I go with her. If Sophia texts, I intercept with a kiss until the phone slides from her hand. She doesn't notice the trade.

When she hesitates—when she says she should study with her group again, or that she misses Sophia—I remind her that danger waits in the shadows. The notes, the stalker, the body in Carter Hall. I make her picture the fear. Then I hold her until she believes only I can keep her safe.

And she thanks me. She thanks me for taking care of her.

She doesn't see the cage. She calls it devotion.

But Professor Hawthorne won't quit.

He stops her after class one day. I hang back, half-hidden by a column.

"You're pale," he says, voice lined with concern. "Are you sleeping? Eating? You look...diminished."

"I'm fine," she insists, clutching her books.

He leans closer. "If you're in trouble, Tesni, you can tell me. You know that, don't you?"

My blood surges hot. Trouble? He wants her to name me. He wants her to confess, to betray.

I stride forward before she can answer, sliding an arm around her waist. "She's fine," I say.

Professor Hawthorne's gaze snaps to mine. He doesn't flinch, not outwardly, but I see the flicker of recognition—he knows exactly what I am.

"Mr. Atthill," he says evenly. "Your reputation precedes you."

"Then you know better than to stand this close to her."

Tesni grips my arm. "Bran—"

But I don't hear her. I hear my father's voice calling me worthless. I hear the crowd cheering when blood hit the ice. I hear every whisper on this campus branding me violent, dangerous, guilty.

And I see Professor Hawthorne's hand resting casually on the desk behind her, too close, too steady.

It happens fast.

I slam him into the wall before I can think, my forearm pressing his chest, my other hand fisted in his shirt. His head thuds against plaster, books sliding from the shelf.

"Stay away from her," I growl, inches from his face. My vision tunnels, rage flooding every vein. "Do you understand me? You so much as say her name again and I'll—"

"Branwen!" Tesni's voice cuts through like a bell.

I freeze, breathing hard. Professor Hawthorne's eyes are wide but not afraid—calculating. He's already thinking about how he'll use this.

I let go, shoving him back. He stumbles but doesn't fall. His expression is cool, composed, like a man who knows the truth is already on his side.

"Thank you for proving my point," he says softly.

Tesni grabs my wrist and pulls me out before I can lunge again. Her grip is small but insistent, dragging me into the hall, into the air that feels too thin.

"Bran, what were you thinking?" she hisses once we're outside.

"He was touching you," I snap.

"He wasn't—" She cuts herself off, pressing a hand to her forehead. "You can't just attack people! You'll get expelled. Arrested. Worse."

"I don't care." I catch her shoulders, forcing her to look at me. "Don't you get it? He wants you. They all want you. I'm the only one who sees it, the only one who'll stop them."

Her eyes glisten, torn between anger and something else—fear? Or love twisted into fear? I can't tell anymore.

"You promised me," I say, softer now, desperation cracking my voice. "You said always. Don't let him take that from us."

She exhales shakily, her hands trembling where they rest against mine. "I'm still here," she whispers. "I'm not leaving."

Relief crashes through me so hard my knees nearly buckle. I pull her into my chest, burying my face in her hair. "I can't lose you. Not now. Not ever."

But even as I hold her, I feel the weight of what I've done pressing down. The look in Professor Hawthorne's eyes. The echo of plaster cracking against his skull.

For the first time, I wonder if I've gone too far.

Not for me. For her.

Because I can bear their hatred. Their suspicion. Even their handcuffs.

But if she looks at me one day and sees only the monster they claim I am—

That, I couldn't survive.

23

Seeking Redemption

Tesni

I'm walking across the quad with a coffee still too hot to drink when two students hurry past, their voices pitched with excitement.

"Did you hear? Atthill went after Professor Hawthorne."

"Yeah, slammed him into a wall. Schultz is already sniffing around."

"Finally. Everyone knew it was only a matter of time."

My legs lock. Coffee sloshes, burning my fingers. I don't feel it.

No. Not Bran.

But the words are everywhere—echoing in classrooms, whispered in the library stacks, painted across the faces of students who glance at me, then away, as if afraid guilt is contagious. By the time I reach my dorm, my hands won't stop shaking.

I find Branwen pacing inside, his hoodie half unzipped, hair damp with sweat. He looks like a storm trapped in human skin.

"He had his hands too close to you," he blurts out before I can speak. "He was baiting me. I just—snapped."

His eyes are wild, begging me to believe, to forgive, to soothe.

But my stomach twists. I can still hear Professor Hawthorne's steady, cultured voice from seminar, can still see the way Branwen's jaw clenched every time my professor said my name. And now Professor Hawthorne has bruises because of it.

"You attacked him," I say softly.

Branwen stops pacing. He stares at me like I've struck him. "I protected you."

I shake my head. "That's not protection, Bran. That's violence. And it doesn't just stay between us—it follows you. It follows me."

For the first time since I met him, I see fear in his eyes. Not fear of punishment, but fear of me slipping through his fingers. He reaches for my arm. "Don't leave. Don't. You said always."

I pull away. "I said it because I wanted to believe you could be different. But now..." My throat tightens. "Now I'm scared."

The word hangs between us like broken glass.

Branwen's face crumples, rage and despair colliding. "I'll fix it," he swears. "I'll prove it to you. Just—don't give up on me."

But for the first time, I'm not sure I have a choice.

I don't sleep. By morning, my decision feels carved in stone: I can't carry this alone anymore.

I text Detective Schultz: *Can we meet?*

His reply is immediate. *Library café. Noon.*

When I arrive, he's already there—suit rumpled, hair silver at the temples, a cup of black coffee steaming in front of him. He looks like he's been waiting for this moment all along.

"Ms. Solaris," he says, motioning me to sit. "I had a feeling we'd talk sooner or later."

I clasp my hands in my lap to hide the tremor. "He went after Professor Hawthorne."

Schultz nods once. "So I hear. Doesn't surprise me. But I'm more interested in what you've seen before that."

I hesitate, then tell him: the violent temper, the controlling grip, the night of the masked figure on the path. Schultz doesn't interrupt, only scribbles in his notebook, his expression unreadable.

When I finish, I brace for condemnation. Instead, he leans back, folding his arms. "You're not crazy. There is another stalker."

The air leaves my lungs. "You believe me?"

"I don't deal in belief. I deal in evidence." He flips a page. "And evidence says there are footprints, camera glitches, timing gaps that don't line up with your boyfriend's movements. Atthill's guilty of plenty, but not everything."

The knot in my chest loosens, but only slightly. "So, Branwen wasn't lying. He really did think someone else was after me."

"He wasn't lying about that," Schultz says carefully. "But don't let that blind you to the rest. He's volatile. Possessive. That's not love, no matter how much you want it to be."

I flinch, but can't deny it. The memory of Branwen's hands slamming Professor Hawthorne into the wall is too vivid.

"What do I do?" I whisper.

"You protect yourself." Schultz's voice is steady, almost gentle. "Start with the basics. Change your routes. Don't walk alone at night. Get pepper spray, keep it where you can reach it. And if he scares you again, you call me. Immediately."

I nod, though the words taste like betrayal.

That afternoon, I stop at a convenience store off campus. The clerk doesn't blink when I ask for pepper spray. He slides it across the counter like gum or pens, everyday protection in a can.

The weight of it in my bag is heavier than I expected. A line I never thought I'd cross.

I start altering my patterns—taking the long way to class, switching study spots, keeping lights on in my room even when I leave. Each change feels like an admission: that I am hunted, not just loved too fiercely.

When Branwen texts, I answer less quickly. When he asks to walk me, I invent excuses. Each lie cuts, but the thought of another outburst, another scene, slices deeper.

At night, I sit on my bed with my journal open, staring at the blank page. In the background, Poppy's "Church Outfit" provides the soundtrack to my inner turmoil. Once, I would have written about Branwen as if he were a hero—dark, flawed, but savable. Now my pen hovers, frozen.

I'm not sure savable is enough anymore.

Schultz calls me two days later. "We traced one of the notes," he says. "The ribbon wasn't from any craft store in town. It's custom, high-end. Same kind Helena Humphries was spotted wearing at a gala last spring."

Helena.

I picture her smirk in the quad, the sharp glint in her eyes when she told me storms don't change. A shiver runs through me.

"So, it really is her," I say.

"It's a lead," Schultz corrects. "Not proof. But it narrows the field."

I thank him and hang up, my mind spinning. Helena, Branwen, shadows and silk. I'm caught between two obsessions, and neither feels like love anymore.

When Branwen comes by that night, he notices the spray on my desk before I can hide it. His face darkens.

"What's that?"

"Protection," I say firmly.

"I told you, you don't need—"

"Yes, I do." My voice is sharp enough to stop him cold. "Because I can't keep pretending everything's fine. You hurt Professor Hawthorne. You scare me sometimes, Bran. And I can't—won't—ignore that anymore."

For a moment, his expression is raw, stricken. Then he looks away, jaw tight. "I'll get better," he mutters. "I'll prove I'm not him."

"I want to believe you," I whisper. "But I can't let belief be my only shield."

The silence that follows is thick, heavy with everything we don't say.

Later, lying awake, I clutch the pepper spray in my hand like a talisman. For the first time since meeting Branwen, I feel the faint outline of a path that doesn't end with me drowning in his storm.

Maybe Schultz is right. Maybe protection doesn't mean choosing sides—it means choosing myself.

And maybe, just maybe, that's the only way to survive.

24

A New Threat

Branwen

Schultz has her number.

I see them through the café glass at noon, his big hands cupped around a paper cup, her shoulders turned in, listening. He's not wearing the hat today; the silver at his temples glints in the window's glare. He looks like a man who takes notes even when the notebook's closed.

He pushes something across the table—a sheet, maybe, or a card—and she nods. He doesn't smile. He doesn't have to. The win is the nod.

When she stands, he stands with her. He puts nothing as heavy as a hand on her shoulder; he uses words instead. That's worse. Hands bruise skin. Words bruise judgment.

My phone buzzes a minute later: *study in north wing. don't wait up.* There's a space where the heart emoji used to be.

So, that's what it is. Alliance. A cop in the room where my name was supposed to be.

Protection, I think, and the word tries to split itself into control. I keep it whole by clenching my jaw.

Her routes are different now. Schultz taught her to change them. I shadow the changes until they feel like old habits. She cuts behind the sculpture garden where the cameras are art, not surveillance. She skips the hellebore path, except when she doesn't. She keeps a small canister on her key ring and her hand learns the weight of it.

Good, part of me says. She's learning.

Not like that, the rest snaps back. Not from him.

I make my rounds before she does. Service doors. Custodial landings. The gap in the dorm camera when the night shift changes. The hinge that screams if you don't lift and push.

From the rink, Hendricks shouts about back-checking. I nod at the right times. On the bench, Evan refuses to meet my eyes, bandage peeking from his wrist where the tape rubbed last game. I am the center of a ring of noise. I move through it untouched.

Tonight, the air is sharp—like busted jagged glass. The lamps hum and throw moth-snow into their halos. I stand where the hellebore bed darkens the path. A ribbon of black silk in my pocket warms to my skin as if it belonged there.

Tesni texts: *home in 10.*

Alone? I ask.

yes. i'm fine.

The word fine is a wall she's learned to build. I lean on it with my shoulder and it holds.

I take the back alleys—where I feel at home. On the dorm's north side a service alcove hides two windows that open badly in summer and not at all in winter unless you know the trick. I found the trick in September when the nights were still soft.

Across the quad, a figure breaks off from the stream of students and slides toward the dorm's shadow. Not big. Not sloppy. Moves like someone who has been watched and learned how to watch back. The coat is dark and expensive, the fabric that remembers the hand that wore it last. The hood is up, but a pale thread escapes near the temple. Not many people on this campus smell like sharp, clean perfume at ten at night.

Helena.

I don't breathe for a count of three. Then I move closer, slipping along the building's lip until the world edits me out.

She doesn't go to the front. She doesn't go to the side door under the camera that blinks tired. She goes to the alcove window two units down from Tesni's. She crouches, gloved fingers on the sill, head cocked. She slides something thin from her pocket—a wedge, a shim, maybe—and works the old latch like she's rehearsed this on a different night, in a different room.

The window lifts a grudging inch. Then two.

She pauses, looks once over each shoulder, not panicked—practiced. A familiar calm. Then she tucks the tool away and tests the metal lip with her weight. Grace in the wrist, economy in the knee. The geometry of a body taught to make lines.

The pane rises. Cold breath spills from the darkness inside. She puts one knee on the sill, tips her center of gravity into the room, and disappears like a name swallowed.

My mouth floods with metal. The world narrows to a square foot of air where the window sighs back into its frame.

I'm already moving. The service door on the north side will stick unless you lift-push. I lift-push. Two steps at a time, heart like a puck ricocheting off boards.

On the landing, a girl in slippers passes me with laundry. She doesn't register me as anything but velocity. I turn into the corridor where Tesni's room sits three doors down, light spilling under the shade like breath.

The hallway is quiet in that studied way dorm hallways are quiet: the quiet of headphones, of late emails, of two people trying to whisper without deciding who should stop first. Far end: exit sign humming. Near: the soft tick of a radiator deciding to be warm.

I don't knock. If Helena is in there, a knock is a courtesy she doesn't get. But I don't walk in, either. The lock will make noise, and so will I. And noise is the one luxury I can't afford if what I need is proof.

Instead, I angle toward the courtyard and the narrow slice of glass that shows her window from outside. The courtyard door gives; the night knifes my cheeks. I move to the spot I found months ago, where the shrubs hide you and the angle is wrong for the cameras. The lamps throw a low wash over the brick; the hellebore bed lifts like a shadow with a heartbeat.

Her window shade is down, but not all the way. There's a sliver of room between fabric and frame. A strip of light. A strip of truth.

A shape crosses that strip, brief as a blink—the curve of a shoulder, the fall of hair, pale where it escapes the hood. Not Tesni. Too poised. Too precise. Then another shape, smaller—the arc of a wrist reaching up, the quick jerk of a hand that knows what it is taking.

My body goes rigid. I can't see faces. I can see intent. A drawer opens—a bar of brightness where its mouth yawns. A hand dips. Something dark glints: ribbon? No. A phone? No. I can't tell. The shade stirs as if a breath brushed it. I bite down until I taste blood.

The shape turns, passes the slit again—profile ghosted, not enough to make a name if you didn't already have one ready. I do. The corner of a mouth like a paper cut. A cheek that looks carved, not soft. The half-second angle of a nose I've watched in lecture halls where she sits five rows up and never leaves early.

Helena.

I should call. I should run. I should lift the sash and haul her out into the cold by the back of her coat like a cat from a counter.

My hands open and close, empty. I think of Schultz in the dark by the quad, the ember of his cigarette marking time. I think of Hendricks saying control yourself or don't come back. I think of Tesni's whisper against my chest: always.

You want evidence, I tell the part of me that is already reaching. You want the clean shape of it so when you break the door down you don't have to explain why.

The shade breathes again. The figure freezes—listening. Then the pane lifts a careful inch. Then two. She slides out backward, small and certain, boots finding the sill without scrape. For half a beat her face is exposed to the lamplight: pale, composed, a statue with secrets.

Her eyes flicker to the courtyard. To the shrubs. To me.

We see each other.

Not a gasp. Not a start. A cool syllable of recognition that doesn't need sound. She pulls the hood forward with one finger, drops lightly, and melts along the wall toward the service alcove, the same route a ghost would choose if it wanted its haunting to look like wind.

My legs remember how to move. I round the bed, the bench, the corner. By the time I hit the alcove, she's gone to ground or out to the quad or into the lights where people turn into witnesses. She knows angles the way I do. She's learned my map and written her own through it.

I stand with my back to the brick, breathing hard. In my pocket, the ribbon heats against my palm until it feels like a coal. Upstairs, behind the shade, a lamp snaps off; the strip of light dies.

Tesni, I think, and my chest constricts until it's a fist.

Schultz taught her to change routes. Good. He didn't teach her who to keep out when the danger wears perfume and knows a hinge.

I look up at the window that is hers. My reflection looks back at me in the glass, a door I promised to be. Every part of me wants to blow it open, flood her with the news that I was right, that the enemy has a name and a face and hands that take in the dark.

Instead, I put my hand on the cold brick and hold it there until the shake leaves.

Protection, I tell myself, and I make it mean waiting for the moment that won't get her hurt.

But the waiting tastes like blood.

So, I stay in the dark. Minutes drag, my pulse counting them louder than the clock tower. The shade above stirs once, twice. Then I hear it: the faint grind of the latch again. She's not gone—she's circling back. The hinge Tesni doesn't know betrays her. By the time it creaks open a second time, I've already moved, already climbing the stairwell. If Helena goes in again, I won't be outside looking up.

25

The Final Stand

Tesni

The air in my dorm feels brittle, charged with something I can't name. The lamp on my desk hums faintly, and the shadows it casts along the walls look deeper than they should. I sit on the bed, pepper spray in my hand, knuckles white around it.

Every instinct in me is screaming to call Schultz, to call Sophia, to call anyone—but instead I wait.

Because if I don't face this, it won't end.

The creak comes soft, almost delicate: the faint grind of the window latch I purposely left unhooked.

The pane slides up, and the room exhales cold.

A figure climbs through in practiced silence. Not Branwen—smaller, sharper, a dancer's precision. When the light touches her face, the breath stutters in my chest.

Helena Humphries.

Her blonde hair has slipped loose from its perfect coil. Her coat drapes around her like a shroud, her perfume sharp in the air. She drops lightly onto the carpet, closes the window behind her, and turns toward me as if she's been invited.

"You," I breathe.

Her smile curves, brittle. "Finally."

I raise the pepper spray just slightly. "Stay there."

Helena tilts her head, amused. "You're not screaming. Interesting."

"I'm done being scared into silence," I say. My voice shakes, but I don't let it falter. "You've been leaving the ribbons. The notes. It was you."

Her eyes glint. "Of course it was. Who else could it be? Branwen, Schultz, all those lumbering men—they can't move through a world quietly. But I can. And you noticed, didn't you?"

The words land heavy. I shake my head. "Why? What do you want from me?"

"What do I want?" She laughs softly, brittle as glass. "You. Only you. From the first day in Professor Hawthorne's seminar, I knew you weren't like the rest. You spoke and made the room listen. I thought—finally. Someone worth watching."

My grip on the spray tightens. "So, you watched me."

"I *studied* you," Helena corrects. "The way you gesture with your sleeve before you say something true. The way you walk faster when you're late, but never cut corners on your sentences. You're not careless. You're extraordinary. And everyone else is too blind to see it."

The words should chill me. They do. But there's something else—pity. She's not a monster in this moment. She's a person collapsing under her own need.

"Helena," I say, forcing calm into my tone. "If you feel that way, you could have just told me. You didn't have to—"

"KILL?" she snaps, her voice slicing the room. Her eyes blaze, and for a moment, the mask slips. "Yes. I killed Mia. Because she was going to ask you out. She told me in the café line—practiced your name, the stupid joke she thought would win you. And you—" Helena's hands tremble, clenched in fists. "You would have said yes because you're kind. Because you don't know how to close doors. And then she would have had you, and I couldn't—"

Her voice breaks into a sob, sharp and startling. "I couldn't let that happen."

I stagger back a step, the spray raised now, heart hammering. "She was my friend," I whisper.

"She was in the way," Helena insists, her voice raw. "I did it for you. For us."

Her eyes are shining, fevered, desperate. And yet I see the cracks—remorse slipping through, panic shadowing her. This is my chance.

"You don't have to keep doing this," I say softly. "You've carried it too long already. Tell Schultz. Tell him everything you told me. He'll listen. You'll still have a chance to choose what happens next."

She shakes her head violently, pacing the room like a caged animal. "Prison? Headlines? My family's name shredded? You don't understand—I'd be destroyed."

"You're destroying yourself already," I reply. "Every note. Every night sneaking through shadows. Every time you climb through a window. You can stop. Right now."

Helena stops pacing, staring at me. Her lips tremble. "You'd stand with me?"

"Yes," I say, truth threading through the fear. "I'll stand with you. I'll tell them you came willingly. That you told me the truth. That you didn't hurt me. You still have control over this story."

For a moment, hope flickers across her face. She almost looks like a student again—polished, poised, someone who could have been just another girl in seminar, not a killer.

But then her expression hardens. "And Branwen?" she asks. Her voice drips disdain. "He staged that ridiculous rescue, didn't he? With Evan in a mask? You really thought you were in danger? He made you a performance, Tesni. I saw it. I smelled the tape adhesive on Evan's hands. Branwen doesn't love you. He cages you."

I flinch, the truth of it cutting close to the bone. But I keep my face calm. "This isn't about him. This is about you and what you've done. And what you're going to do next."

Her chest heaves, panic and fury twisting her features. "You're calm," she whispers, astonished. "Even now."

"I'm tired," I say. "Of being watched. Of being cornered. Of losing people I care about. Please, Helena. End this before it ends you."

Silence stretches. Her gaze flickers to the spray in my hand, then back to my eyes. Slowly, carefully, she exhales. "All right. I'll come."

Relief floods me, knees almost giving way. "Thank you."

"Not for you," she mutters. "For me. I'm tired, too."

I nod. "We'll go to Schultz. Tonight."

She glances at the door. "Yes. Before anyone stops us—"

The handle jerks.

The door slams open so hard the lamp rattles.

Branwen storms inside, eyes blazing, shoulders squared like a battering ram. His gaze lands on Helena, then on me, then back to her, fury radiating from every line of him.

"You," he snarls.

Helena straightens, smirk twisting her lips again. "Of course."

Branwen takes a step forward. "Get away from her."

"Bran—" I start, raising a hand.

But he doesn't hear me. His eyes are locked on Helena, his rage boiling over. And Helena, instead of shrinking, lets out a laugh that chills me to my bones.

The fragile calm I built shatters. I see her hand dart inside her coat—something metallic glinting. A knife.

Everything erupts at once.

26

Love and Madness

Branwen

The glint of steel flashes before I can blink.

Helena moves fast—faster than I thought possible—but fear sharpens my reflexes. I lunge sideways, pulling Tesni behind me as the blade slices past. It screeches against the wall, sparks flying, the sound like teeth on glass.

"You think you can steal her from me?" Helena hisses, eyes wild, voice broken and beautiful in its fury. "You think she was ever yours?"

She slashes again. This time the knife kisses my arm, a searing line of fire opening along muscle. I grunt, pain ripping through me, but I plant my feet. Blood runs hot down my sleeve.

Tesni screams my name, but I can't look at her. All I see is Helena—the rival, the shadow, the girl who moved through the night like a phantom while I blamed myself.

"You killed Mia," I snarl. "You left her like trash in that lounge."

"She was in the way," Helena spits. "Just like you are."

She lunges again, and I catch her wrist. The knife trembles between us, quivering like a live thing. Her strength surprises me—desperation makes her fierce. My wound weakens me, blood soaking my hoodie, but rage keeps me steady.

Our bodies crash against the desk, books scattering. Tesni's lamp topples and clatters, plunging half the room into shadow. Helena twists, aiming for my throat. I wrench the blade away by inches, teeth gritted, breath hot in her face.

"You don't love her," she rasps. "You want to own her."

"And you don't?" I snarl back.

For a moment, our eyes lock—mirror images of obsession, distorted in different shapes.

She knees me hard, and the knife rips free. Pain explodes as the blade slices my side. I stagger, clutching my ribs. Helena bolts for the door.

"Bran!" Tesni shouts, reaching for me.

I shake my head. "Stay here."

And then I run.

The night air punches me in the lungs as I burst onto the quad. Helena's coat flares behind her like a banner as she sprints across the frost-streaked lawn. I follow, my wound leaving a crimson trail in the pale light.

She heads for the river—the path dips, slopes, mud slick under scattered leaves. I know it before she does: the bank here is treacherous, the edge crumbling.

"Stop!" I shout, voice raw. "It's over!"

She glances back, hair flying loose, eyes blazing with something close to triumph. "It's never over," she spits, and pushes harder.

I close the distance, feet pounding, every step agony. My vision narrows, blood loss making the world tilt. The roar of the river swells in my ears.

She stumbles on a root, recovers, then skids on wet ground. Her arms pinwheel. The knife flashes once, then tumbles from her grip into the dark.

I lunge, reaching for her hand. Fingers brush skin—slippery, desperate.

"Got you!" I rasp.

But the earth gives way beneath her boots. Her scream splits the night as the bank collapses. My grip slips. I claw at her sleeve, catch nothing but fabric tearing.

And then she's gone.

Her body plummets into the churning black below. The river seizes her, swallows her whole. The current pulls fast, merciless. One second she's there, thrashing, pale hair catching moonlight. The next, nothing.

Only the roar of water.

I stand frozen at the edge, chest heaving, blood soaking my side. My hand still reaches into emptiness.

I meant to catch her. I meant to stop this.

But she's gone.

Shock drags me backward, stumbling on weak legs. The world feels muffled, unreal. I press my palm to my wound; it comes away slick, red, shining in the cold.

Behind me, boots crunch. A voice cuts through the ringing in my ears. "Atthill."

I turn. Detective Schultz steps out of the trees, coat collar high, cigarette ember dying between his fingers. His eyes take in the scene—the blood, the knife in the dirt, the ruined bank, the black water swallowing secrets.

"She's gone," I rasp.

"I saw," he says simply. His face is unreadable, neither triumphant nor shocked. Just tired.

Tesni runs up behind him, breathless, her cry breaking when she sees me. "Bran!" She reaches for me, but Schultz blocks her gently with one arm.

"Stay back," he warns. His gaze never leaves mine. "You need a hospital."

I stagger, shaking my head. "No. I need—"

"What?" Schultz presses. "Revenge? Another fight? You think this ends if you keep swinging?"

My knees threaten to buckle. "I tried to save her."

"I know," he says. "And I also know you nearly hospitalized Professor Hawthorne, terrified half this campus, and just bled yourself out chasing a girl into a river." He steps closer, voice steady, low. "This is your tipping point, Atthill. You keep down this road, you'll bury Tesni along with everyone else."

Tesni whispers my name again, eyes wide with fear—not of Helena, not of Schultz. Of me.

The sight guts me worse than the knife.

Schultz puts a hand on my shoulder, firm, grounding. "I'll let you walk away from this tonight. Helena's gone. But only on one condition."

My vision blurs, pain roaring. "What?"

"You get help," he says flatly. "Real help. Anger, obsession, all of it. You don't, and next time, no one walks away. Not her. Not you."

The words sink like stones. I look at Tesni—her trembling hands, her lips pressed tight against tears. The promise she whispered days ago—always—feels fragile now, frayed.

My body sways. The river roars behind me.

Finally, I nod. "Okay."

Schultz exhales, releasing a tension I hadn't seen. "Good. Now let's get you stitched before you pass out."

I stumble forward, and this time it's Tesni who catches me, her small frame bracing mine. For a moment, her arms are the only thing holding me upright.

But her eyes—her eyes are different.

And I know nothing will ever be the same.

3. 27

Aftermath

Tesni

The campus feels quieter, but not safer.

In the days since that night by the river, the air has carried an edge—as if everyone is breathing more carefully, waiting for something else to break. People whisper in corners, their voices bending around names they don't want to say aloud. Branwen. Helena. Mine.

I walk across the quad and catch fragments.

"—missing still?"

"They say she fell—"

"—Atthill's fault—"

The words sting, but I keep walking. I've spent too much time swallowed by what other people think.

Sophia waits for me at the café, fingers tapping nervously on her cup. I almost turn back, afraid she'll look through me the way she did before. But when she sees me, her eyes soften.

"Tesni," she says, and her voice cracks.

I sit down before I lose the nerve. For a moment, neither of us speaks. Then Sophia reaches across the table and grips my hand.

"I'm sorry," she says. "I should have been there. I knew something was wrong, and I—"

Tears sting my eyes. "You tried. I didn't listen."

We squeeze each other's hands until the silence turns into something else—not accusation, but forgiveness.

She studies me, her gaze steady. "How are you...really?"

I swallow. "Shaken. Tired. Afraid of what I almost let myself believe was love."

Sophia nods slowly, her thumb brushing over my knuckles. "You're here. That's what matters. We'll figure out the rest."

I start counselling a week later—per the administration's advice. The first session feels strange, like learning a new language. The therapist asks gentle questions: How did you feel when the notes appeared? What did you tell yourself to survive? What do you need now?

For once, I don't try to give the "right" answers. I say the messy truths: that I thought I was strong enough to fix him, that I mistook obsession for devotion, that part of me still aches when I think of Branwen's voice whispering always.

"Love and fear can feel similar in the body," the therapist says. "But they aren't the same. Learning the difference is part of healing."

Her words lodge deep.

Afterward, I walk across campus with the pepper spray still on my key ring. The lamps flicker as evening settles in, but I don't feel as paralyzed as before. Fear is still there—but now it's a signal, not a chain.

Sophia and I meet more often. Sometimes we talk about Helena—her brilliance, her sharpness, how none of us saw the fracture lines beneath her composure. Sometimes we don't talk at all, just sit with our coffees and let the silence be soft.

Nora joins us once, tentative, as if unsure she's welcome. She is. Together, we try to stitch something back from the pieces.

It isn't perfect. Some nights I still wake with Branwen's voice echoing in my head, or Helena's eyes flashing in the lamplight. But when I do, I text Sophia. And she answers.

Part of me wants to run—transfer, start fresh somewhere my name isn't murmured in corridors. Somewhere people don't look at me and see a cautionary tale.

But another part of me wants to stay. To reclaim UC Wisteria as more than a crime scene. To finish what I started, not for Branwen, not for Helena, but for myself.

"Think about what you need, not what anyone else expects," Sophia tells me when I bring it up.

So I think. I make lists. Stay or go. Heal or hide. Neither answer feels easy.

But for the first time, I let myself believe that choosing for myself is possible.

28

Redemption's Path

Branwen

The first time I sit in the therapy circle, I want to bolt.

The chairs are cheap metal, the kind that scrape on linoleum. A pot of coffee sits in the corner, burnt and bitter. The clock ticks loud enough to make my teeth grind.

I'm used to noise—crowds chanting my name, skates slicing ice, fists pounding helmets. This quiet feels worse. Too sharp. Too honest.

The therapist, a woman with gray streaks in her braid, says, "We share when we're ready." She looks at me. Not unkind. Just steady.

I look away.

Around the circle, voices unravel. A man talks about smashing a door when his wife forgot the rent. A woman describes hiding bottles in her closet. A college kid admits he can't stop driving too fast, even after the accident.

The words hang in the air, heavy but unpunished.

When it's my turn, I mutter, "Pass."

No one argues. That almost unnerves me more.

The second session, I say three words: "I get angry."

The group nods. They wait, but I stop there.

The third session, I add, "I hurt people." The silence that follows is worse than judgment. It's understanding.

By the fourth, I'm telling them about the ice, about the fight, about the boy who taunted me and how I wanted him not to wake up. About Professor Hawthorne's smirk, Helena's knife, the sound of the river swallowing her whole.

I expect the room to flinch. Instead, one guy across the circle says, "I know what it's like when rage feels bigger than your body."

Something loosens in me. A crack in the armor.

Weeks pass. The therapist keeps asking the same question: "What do you want that isn't control?"

At first, I don't know. Then one night I dream of a rink filled with kids, skates clumsy, sticks too long, laughter echoing off boards. No pressure. No scouts. Just joy.

When I wake, the answer feels like oxygen.

I sign up to help with the youth hockey program at the community center. Hendricks puts in a word despite everything—maybe because he knows what the ice can do for a kid who feels too angry to breathe.

The first night, ten boys and girls wobble across the rink, helmets askew, cheeks flushed. They fall, laugh, scramble up again.

One boy, Jamie, refuses to get off the bench. His arms are crossed, his eyes dark.

"I'm gonna fall," he mutters when I crouch beside him.

"You will," I say. "That's the point."

He frowns. "You like falling?"

"No," I admit. "But I like getting up."

He thinks about that. Five minutes later, he's on the ice. *Part* of it.

By the end of practice, his grin makes my chest ache in a way fighting never did.

Therapy changes, too. I start to talk about more than fists and ice. I talk about my father's voice in my head, telling me worth equals violence. I talk about my mother's silence, a wound that never scabbed.

The therapist says, "You're rewriting the story."

I'm not sure yet. But for the first time, I want to try.

At night, I still think of Tesni.

Her voice whispering always. Her eyes widening when I scared her. Her hands trembling when she chose to stay.

I don't text her. I don't wait outside her dorm. I don't stalk the paths I memorized.

Instead, I lace up skates and chase kids across the ice. I sit in therapy and say words that taste like rust. I try to build a version of myself that isn't built on rage.

I don't know if she'll ever forgive me.

But I know this: one day, if I can keep standing up after every fall, maybe I'll be someone worthy of her trust.

Until then, I skate. I speak. I try.

29

New Beginnings

Tesni

The campus feels *really* different now.

It's not that the shadows have vanished, or that whispers don't still ripple when I walk across the quad. But the weight pressing down on me is lighter. Maybe it's because I've finally chosen to stop carrying everyone else's storms.

Classes have resumed their rhythm—papers, deadlines, Professor Hawthorne's seminar where I sit straighter now, speaking without the need for anyone's approval. My grades are steady. My thoughts are steadier.

But healing isn't just grades and essays. It's faces. So, I begin with Sophia.

We sit in the library, our heads bent together like we did before all of this. She cracks a joke about how she'd stalk *coffee* if it ever tried to get away from her, and I laugh harder than I thought I could. For the first time in months, laughter doesn't feel like betrayal.

When Nora joins us, I let her. When new friends drift into our circle, I welcome them. Bit by bit, my world expands beyond Branwen's shadow and Helena's gaze.

The idea for the support group comes late one night when I can't sleep. I think about all the girls who walk back to their dorms clutching keys like weapons, about the boy who whispered in group therapy that his roommate shoved him, about the silence that isolates.

What if silence didn't win?

By mid-semester, a dozen of us gather weekly in a classroom we've claimed with donated tea and a hand-painted sign: Voices Rising. Survivors, allies, anyone who needs to speak. We share stories. We cry. We laugh. We sit in the kind of silence that feels like safety, not fear.

I'm not sure I lead as much as I hold space. But holding space is its own kind of power.

The invitation to speak comes in an email stamped with the dean's signature. Student Forum on Personal Safety and Empowerment. Would I consider giving the keynote?

I stare at the screen for a long time, my chest tight.

Then I write back: *Yes.*

The auditorium is packed the night of the event—rows of students, faculty, even a handful of parents. The stage lights are hot on my face, but my palms stay dry. For once, I don't feel small behind a podium.

I tell them what I've learned: that danger doesn't always wear a mask, that love and control are not the same, that speaking out is not weakness but survival. I talk about Mia—her kindness, her laughter—and how remembering her means refusing to let fear silence us.

The words rise steadier than I imagined. I see nods in the crowd. I see tears. I see hope.

And then, halfway back in the audience, I see him.

Branwen.

He sits very still, hands clasped, eyes fixed on me. His shoulders are less rigid than I remember, his expression stripped of swagger. There's no storm in his gaze, only quiet.

My voice almost falters. Almost. But then I keep going, finishing with the line that has become my mantra: "Safety isn't something we're given. It's something we claim."

The applause swells like a tide.

Afterward, in the lobby, people crowd around me with thanks and questions. I smile, I answer, I accept hugs. And then I see him again, waiting at the edge of the room. Not pushing forward. Just waiting.

Our eyes meet. For a moment, the months collapse—hellebore ribbons, whispered always, the roar of the river.

I walk toward him.

"Tesni," he says, his voice low, careful.

"Branwen."

He looks thinner, older somehow. A small scar peeks from under his sleeve where Helena's knife found him. "I wanted to hear you speak," he says. "You were...incredible."

I study him, searching for the old sharpness, the desperation. It isn't there. What I see instead is humility.

He swallows. "I owe you more than words, but I'll start here. I'm sorry. For everything. For hurting you, for scaring you, for thinking love meant possession. Therapy's teaching me how much I don't know. But I'm trying. Every day."

His voice cracks, and he doesn't try to hide it.

For a long moment, I just look at him, the boy who almost drowned me and the man who is learning to stand.

"I see the change," I say softly. "I don't know what it means yet. But I see it."

He nods, acceptance in the gesture. He doesn't push, doesn't demand.

And because of that—because he finally leaves the choice to me—I take a breath and say, "Maybe we can try again. Slowly. Carefully. On my terms."

Hope flickers across his face, fragile and real. "I'd like that," he whispers.

We stand in the hum of voices and footsteps, a cautious bridge stretching between us. Not a cage. Not a storm. Something entirely new.

Epilogue: Seeds of Change

Tesni

The winter finally broke.

Where snow once bent the hellebore beds into silence, new shoots push through, green and stubborn. I kneel on the edge of the quad, dirt under my nails, sweat beading across my brow. Around me, volunteers from Voices Rising laugh and chatter as we plant row after row of hellebores—white, pink, even dark purple. Not as warnings this time, not as shadows. As symbols.

A field of resilience.

I press one seedling into the earth and smooth the soil over its roots. Growth is never instant, never easy, but with care, it takes hold. That's what I'm learning. That's what I'm living.

Life has changed in small but steady ways. Sophia and I are closer than ever; she comes to every meeting of the support group, sometimes just to pour tea, sometimes to share, always to remind me that friendship can be rebuilt. Her presence steadies me, the way it always did.

And sometimes, when my mind drifts, it finds Professor Hawthorne. I hear whispers that the administration is looking into him again—something about another female student, the kind of rumor that burns hotter for being half-hidden. I should dismiss it, but instead I feel a flicker I don't want to name. Jealousy. The truth is, I still think of him with a kind of fondness I can't scrub away, and I hate how easily I picture his perfect smile in the glow of a lecture hall. Part of me wonders if, someday, our paths might cross in a way that isn't all shadows and warnings.

Our group has grown. We started with a dozen; now, nearly fifty gather each week. Stories spill into the circle—painful, hopeful, unfinished. Each one matters. Each one proves that silence can be broken.

And Branwen—he's still here, but different.

He goes to therapy three times a week. He volunteers at the youth hockey rink, teaching kids how to skate, how to fall, how to get up again. Sometimes he tells me about a boy who reminds him of himself, all rage and elbows, and I can see pride flicker in his eyes when he says the boy is learning to channel that energy into speed, not fists.

He hasn't asked me to define what we are. He just shows up, steady and quiet, letting me decide how close or far we stand. That patience is new. That patience is proof.

Tonight, after everyone leaves, I walk back across the quad. The new hellebores are tucked into the earth like promises. Branwen waits at the far end, hands in his pockets, watching.

For a moment, as I approach, something in his gaze sharpens. A flash of the old storm—the boy who once thought love meant possession. My chest tightens.

But then he exhales, and his expression softens. He reaches out—not to grab, not to cage. Just to brush a strand of hair from my cheek, his touch light, almost reverent.

"Proud of you," he murmurs.

It's simple. Warm. Enough.

I smile, feeling the soil still clinging to my hands, the weight of everything I've lived through.

This isn't a fairy tale. But it's real. And for now, that's all I need.

LOVE IT? Please leave a review:
https://aberstoatpublishing.com/hellebore-fields

LISTEN: Songs mentioned in the boook.